First Comes Courage

by
Robert Edmond Alter

WILDSIDE PRESS

CONTENTS

Author's Note

In a few instances in these accounts of true events I have resorted to invented dialogue where it seems obvious what the people involved would have said.   R.E.A.

1 THE RED FORT

Colonel George Campbell of the 52nd stared searchingly, almost compassionately, at the two young engineer officers at the other end of the mess table. Then he stood up and raised his drinking cup.

"Gentlemen, I give you Lieutenants Home and Salkeld," he said.

"Lieutenants Home and Salkeld!" all the officers echoed.

The two young lieutenants being honored, Duncan Home and Philip Salkeld, sat in mute embarrassment, smiling at each other across the table. They were gratified by the toast, of course, but there was something about their identical fixed smiles which bore a trace of unadmitted apprehension.

They had just volunteered for a suicide mission.

The colonel resumed his seat, saying with forced wryness, "Shouldn't wonder you'll both be receiving

9

one of those new medals they're sending out from England. The Victoria Cross."

Everyone turned to Home and Salkeld and began to make congratulatory sounds—though they all secretly believed that the only way the two lieutenants would receive the V.C. would be posthumously. And, secretly, Home and Salkeld believed the same thing.

It was the night of September 12, 1857. Four months before, on May 10, the violent Sepoy Mutiny had erupted in India, turning the vast land into a battlefield where no quarter was asked and none given.

The Sepoys ("Pandies" the British called them) were the Indian soldiers who had served the British East India Trading Company for decades. There had been an expanding discontent among these troops for a number of years, marked infrequently by isolated incidences of open rebellion and violence, but the British had preferred to ignore the warning signs.

The Sepoys' deepest concern was that the British were trying to abolish their traditional caste system; and when the Company issued the new Lee-Enfield rifles to the Indian Army in the spring of 1857, it also issued a new type of paper cartridge supposedly greased with cow's fat and pig's lard. Cows were sacred to the Hindus and pigs were abhorred by the Muhammadans.

This incident was enough to ignite the powder keg of dissension. It pushed the 257,000 Sepoys of both religions over the brink of rebellion.

The mutineers first arose in arms at Meerut, a British post forty miles north of Delhi. They ran wild—shooting, sabering, bayoneting everyone in their path.

Meerut was turned into a screaming slaughterhouse, and the British—men, women, and children—were butchered like helpless sheep. The post was gutted and burned, and the triumphant and blood-mad Sepoys rode out of Meerut to make for Delhi.

The palace of the octogenarian Shah Bahadur, an Indian ruler who opposed the British, was in the old city of Delhi—called the Red Fort because of its red sandstone walls—and mutinous Sepoys from all of India turned to this rallying point with a natural instinct.

Geographically and militarily this vast rat-warren of minarets, mosques, and slums was ideal. The city was surrounded by seven miles of tall thick walls guarded by inclines, escarps, moats, bastions, and cannon. Let the British come if they dared!

They came.

By the end of June there were 40,000 Sepoys inside the city. Outside the walls was a British force of 6,000. Incredibly, these mere 6,000 soldiers managed to besiege Delhi. Every day a howling horde of Sepoys rushed through the gates to drive the British away— and every day the British doggedly forced them back into the city.

The siege dragged on for over three months; attack and counterattack, the siege guns hammering night and day at the Red Fort, and the Sepoy guns slamming back at the British assault trenches and breastworks facing the city.

All roads and plains for miles around were cluttered with the bloated, putrid carcasses of work elephants, horses, and men. Nobody did anything about them.

There were no burial parties. The stench was over-powering and fat flies buzzed by the millions. Dysentery and fever were widespread.

Everybody in the British camp had the same thought; Assault. *When are we going to storm Delhi?* But General Wilson was haunted with apprehension and indecision. He stalled for reinforcements, and when they finally arrived there were only 3,000 of them.

The general's total force was now 8,748. On paper. Three thousand of these troops were on sick call.

Understandably, the harassed general attempted to delay his decision. But his persistent, combat-eager officers were too much for him. Finally they pressured him to attack and he agreed.

"Very well. I believe it is doomed to fail, but we will attempt it. We will storm the city on September thirteenth. The morning of September thirteenth. . . ."

Three A.M., and Home and Salkeld crawled out of their cots. Salkeld swallowed his castor oil and opium drops, which had been prescribed for the dysentery and fever.

"Want some?" he asked his friend.

Home shook his head. He had good reason to believe he wasn't going to live long enough to catch a disease. He brushed aside a swarm of early morning flies and selected two lucifer matches, broke one in half, and arranged the heads evenly in his closed fist.

"Long match leads the first squad of Sappers to the gate," he said. "Short match takes the second squad and lights the fuse."

Salkeld drew the short match.

"Bad luck," Home said. "But if I can get my men in there fast enough, maybe we can catch Pandy (Sepoy) off-guard and give you a chance to do your job before they realize what we're up to."

Salked nodded. He was thinking how ironic their situation was. Four months ago he and Home had been trapped inside Delhi on the day the mutiny began. They had had a frightful time fighting their way out through the Kashmir Gate. Today they were going to have a worse time getting *into* the city, again by the same gate.

They left their tent to round up the volunteer party of Sappers. (The military engineers of that time who laid mines were called sappers.) There were nine of them. Three British sergeants from the Bengal Sappers —Carmichael, Burgess, and Smith; four Indian Sappers, and a *havildar* (sergeant major); and a bugler named Hawthorne.

"You understand our job," Home said to them. "Each man will carry a twenty-five-pound bag of gunpowder. As soon as the first two assault columns strike the west wall, we will run to the Kashmir Gate in the north wall and plant our charges. Hawthorne will give the signal as soon as the breach is blown so that Colonel Campbell's assault column can come through."

He then selected the *havildar*, the bugler, and two of the native Sappers for the first squad. The British batteries, which had been pounding Delhi's walls all night, began firing with redoubled fury.

"That means they're covering the advance of our

troops," Home said. "Time for us to go." He and Salkeld shook hands.

"See you in Delhi," Salkeld said, smiling.

Home smiled back. Neither of them believed it.

The first two assault columns had already started across the pre-dawn darkened plain and were already having trouble. Some three hundred and sixty sick men had crawled from their beds to join the great assault, and many of them were dropping in their tracks, burning with fever.

"No sick or wounded of any rank are to be picked up by anyone in the ranks!" the officers shouted. "Leave them where they are. They'll be picked up by the *doolie*-bearers if possible. If not—then they'll just have to take their chances with the Pandies!"

Grim news for the storming parties. Pandy wasn't admired as an administer of first aid. But every soldier understood that the assaulting columns were already too fantastically small to spare a single man for Good Samaritan duty.

Delhi was returning the fire with everything it had, lashing the air with grape and canister, sending howling roundshot across the plain, crisscrossing the pallid sky with rockets and Greek fire, lighting up the dark with livid flashes.

The British batteries grumbled into silence and the 60th Rifles cheered and surged toward the west moat. Men with bamboo scaling ladders met a withering fire at the top of the incline, and they fell in clumps, writhing and screaming and rolling down the counterscarp. The only covering fire they had was from the

Rifles, who were already in the ditch and in trouble themselves.

In the first ten minutes a hundred men fell as they tried to bridge the moat. The storming parties were too excited to wait. They rushed forward and took the places of the ladder-men who had fallen. Men toppled and slid into the ditch, others leaped down and waded over the bodies, dragging the ladders as they went.

The Sepoys rained musket fire on them from the blood-red walls, and flung down rocks and stones and tiles, but there was something inexorable and awesome about the storming Britons. They scrambled and tumbled and fell, but they refused to be forced back.

Cursing and yelling, they scrabbled over the inner ledge and up the shell-pocked walls. A soldier named Arthur Lang climbed hand-over-hand up the splintered stone curtain, lost his balance, and started to topple backward onto the sharp points of the close-packed bayonets below him. Two Gurkhas who didn't even belong to his squad caught him just in time to save him from being impaled by his own men.

Captain Julius Medley stopped a musket ball with his right arm and was nearly knocked from his ladder, but he was in such an emotional frenzy he didn't even realize it. He went on up and over with his useless arm dangling and dripping at his side.

And nineteen-year-old Lieutenant Edward Vibart found a breach in the wall and led his yelling men in. A Sepoy bullet clipped his sword blade an inch from the hilt and nearly tore it from his hand. He heard the

soldier who was standing directly behind him shout:
"Thank you, sir! That saved *me!*"

Forty ladder-men had led the spearhead, and thirty of them were now dead or dying or wounded in the ditch. The rest of the assault was going up and over the wall and into the city. The situation was looking very good on the west wall. But the north wall was another story. . . .

Duncan Home's Sapper squad took off at the appointed time.

Home and the bugler led the way, running with their heads down as they weathered the hissing hail of musket balls. They zagged a little to give Pandy a poor target, but the twenty-five pounds of gunpowder each of them lugged tended to make their movements awkward.

Theirs was the most dangerous task of the entire assault and none of them expected to survive. It was not heroics that drew them toward the bullet-whipped moat; they were British soldiers and they believed this was their duty. It was as simple as that.

The bullets were cutting the dried weeds in the parched dirt around Home's running feet. He started to cheer as he ran, and the others picked it up, and then they were all cheering as they raced toward the moat in extended order.

In that last lung-bursting rush to the edge of the counterscarp, with the Sepoy muskets firing at him, Home kept his eyes on the great red wall dead ahead and saw the gawking faces of the Sepoys staring through the loopholes.

The Kashmir Gate was inset in a stone trench, and Home thought that if he could just reach it he would be safe inside the recess. He nearly groaned when he suddenly saw that the gate's wooden drawbridge had been shattered by shellfire. A few jagged crossbeams, a clutter of splintered planking was all that was left of it.

Hastily stepping and jumping from one torn plank to the next, he led his men over the twenty-five-foot-wide moat that yawned under them. The huge gate loomed ahead, and Home scampered for it like a frightened child toddling to the outstretched safety of his mother's arms.

The gate had a small grilled wicket on one side, and that meant the Sepoys could stand inside the wicket and take potshots at them as they tried to set up their powder charges!

Switching hands with the powder bag, Home drew his pistol as he took the last leap across the gaping planks—cocked the hammer and braced his legs as he swung around to face the wicket.

The startled face of a musket-bearing Sepoy appeared behind the grill, and Home fired point-blank. The pistol kicked high in his hand as the Sepoy's face vanished in the swirl of smoke. Home quickly banked his powder bag against the foot of the gate.

Good. That was the first out of ten. Then the bugler was beside him, tugging at his shoulder and yelling.

"We can't st'y 'ere, Leftenant! The Pandies will blast us to pie through the wicket!"

The Sepoy fire was not only coming from the wicket but through the loopholes and from the top of the gate as well. Bullets hummed and flattened and whined off the masonry around them. But Home couldn't seek cover until he had his squad's bags set up and ready for the second squad.

He wanted to run so badly he was ready to scream. But he couldn't, and he knew it. He had to think of Salkeld and his men.

The *havildar* blundered into the recess and stiffened like a petrified man, his mouth flying open in astonishment. He cried, "*Sahib!*" and thrust his powder bag at Home, and fell over the loose planking and into the ditch with a bullet in his hip.

Home turned with the *havildar's* powder bag and set it in place, thinking, *That's two.* He yelled at the bugler.

"Get out of this! That's an order!"

They couldn't afford to lose the bugler because he was the man who had to bring on Campbell's assault column. But Hawthorne was one of those stubborn soldiers who refuse to leave a good officer.

"No sir! Not till you're bloody well ready to go!"

Home's two native Sappers came piling into the recess in a frenzy of excitement, dumped their bags, and turned back in utter confusion, wondering where to seek cover. Home and the bugler arranged the bags against the timber gate.

"Take cover in the moat!" Home yelled as he straightened up.

One of the Indian Sappers doubled over with a bullet in his stomach and plunged into the ditch. Home, Hawthorne, and the other Sapper leaped from the splintery drawbridge into the moat.

The moat was at least fifteen feet deep. There was no water—only a hard crust of dry mud. The three men felt the jolt of their fall all through their bodies.

Bewilderedly, they helped each other under the partial shelter of the drawbridge which looked like a span of lacework. Bullets hit the dirt around them. The Sapper who had been shot was dying. The *havildar* had his head on his arms, his face in the mud. He was still alive but not by much of a margin. His fall had broken something inside him and he could feel the bleeding.

"We've completely lost the element of surprise!" Home raged helplessly. *"Salkeld is in for it now!"*

He was indeed. But he had drawn the short straw and there was nothing to do except to go through with the attack as planned. The powder bags had to be lighted and he was holding the portfire.

Salkeld drew his sword and pointed it at the gate, his teeth flashing at the three British sergeants and the two native Sappers.

"Here we go then!" he cried.

They charged forward with the second lot of bags. The Sepoys on the red walls definitely knew what was happening by now and they threw out a hissing sheet of musketry to halt the Sappers.

Salkeld went hopping across the drawbridge with his little squad of desperate men. One of the Sappers was hit flush in the face and he sprawled on the ruptured planks. The second Sapper paused to snatch up his comrade's powder bag and he caught a bullet in the hip. He went to his knees and held up both powder bags.

Carmichael grabbed one of them and Burgess got the other, as the wounded Sapper rolled over the edge and dropped into the ditch.

Carmichael was the first to reach the gate. He crouched over to arrange both powder bags alongside the ones Home's squad had left. Salkeld and Burgess stumbled into the recess together—just as a Sepoy fired a musket through the wicket at Carmichael. Sergeant Carmichael spun halfway around, clutched at the hot smoky air, and fell dead at Salkeld's feet.

Sergeant Smith was the last man of the explosion party to cross the skeletal drawbridge, and by the time he reached the gate every many except Salkeld and Burgess was either wounded or dead or down in the ditch.

Smith dumped his bag by the others and reached for one of Carmichael's which had tilted aside. Burgess was firing his rifle and the lieutenant's pistol through the smoke-clogged wicket. The air around the three huddled Britons was so thick with Sepoy bullets that the red stones of the walls seemed to be in some amazing process of continuous, yet static disintegration.

But they were so closely pressed inside the recess that the Sepoys couldn't hit them. Furious Pandies were lunging out of the loopholes and nearly toppling off the walls in their eagerness to shoot the Englishmen before they could light the fuse.

Salkeld, pressing as tightly against the wooden framework of the gate as he could get, had his left leg stretched out behind him for balance. A Sepoy behind the grilled wicket spotted the lieutenant's leg and fired a bullet into it just as Salkeld started to apply his slow match to the fuse.

Salkeld bucked up in pain, took an aimless step away from the gate and felt a red wash of vertigo rush through him. His leg buckled under him and he went down to his knees and started to tip off the drawbridge. Blindly, he shoved the slow match toward Burgess.

"Take it!" he gasped, and rolled over the edge.

Sergeant Burgess grabbed the portfire mechanically and set it to the fuse. Nothing happened. No sputter or spark.

"It won't go off!" he cried. "The match 'as gone out!"

Sergeant Smith, standing tightly against the gate, pulled out a box of lucifer matches and shoved them at Burgess. " 'Ere you go, myte," he said.

Burgess reached for the matches but didn't complete the gesture. A bullet hit him and he spun around and went over backward after the lieutenant into the ditch.

Smith, alone now, kneeled down and struck a match and sheltered the little peak of flame in his hand. He fed it to the frayed end of the fuse. The fuse caught like a firecracker with a hiss and a spurt of smoke, and Smith recoiled in horror. The temperamental fuse was going to go off right in his face!

He snatched up his rifle, scrambled around in a crouch and jumped off the drawbridge, and was still in midair when—

The red wall of the fort seemed to buckle. The powder bags exploded with a Gargantuan blast that knocked dozens of howling mutineers flat. Smith was caught in the explosion, lifted and flung forward into space. . . .

He landed crumpled at the bottom of the ditch, with falling stones, shards of masonry, and wood splinters raining over him. Powder-burned and with a bruise on one leg, he sat up and looked around, too stunned to even be surprised that he was still alive.

Home, Hawthorne, and the last Sapper were groping about in the choking dust and smoke, anxiously calling each other's names, none of them wanting to discover that he had been left alone in that pit. Home had started to go to Salkeld's aid when the explosion occurred. Now he was dazed and lost in the gloom.

Smith fumbled blindly along the ledge of the wall and bumped into Home. They were standing over Burgess' body. The wounded Sapper was dying just behind them. The smoke drifted off and they saw Salkeld lying in the middle of the ditch, half buried under rubble and dust. His arms and legs were moving feebly.

Now that the smoke had cleared, the Pandies up on the walls could see the survivors of the explosion party and they opened fire again. Sergeant Smith and Bugler Hawthorne darted out and picked up Salkeld and hauled him under the drawbridge.

When they had dragged him out of the line of musket fire, Lieutenant Salkeld sprawled against some stones. His wounded leg stuck out awkwardly and he had a broken arm from his fall. He stared straight ahead at the counterscarp with a strange glassy expression. He was in deep shock.

"Go on back to the column, sir, with the bugler," Smith said to Home. "I'll st'y 'ere with the leftenant and the rest."

"No," Home said. "We'll all stick it together. Sound the charge, Bugler."

Hawthorne stood up with his dusty bugle and blew the advance, but the ceaseless roar of the mortars and musketry was so overpowering that Home doubted if Campbell's column could hear the call. Crouching among his dead and dying comrades, red with dust and blood, with Pandy bullets hitting the baked mud around them, Home closed his eyes in sick desperation.

He was certain that Campbell would never hear the bugle from the bottom of the moat. There might be a chance of it, though, if the bugle was blown from the counterscarp. But he couldn't order Hawthorne to try a deadly job like that. . . .

"Give me that!" he said, snatching the bugle from Hawthorne and starting to run with it across the floor of the moat.

"Come back, Leftenant! They'll shoot you dead!"

They probably would, but it had to be done, Home thought as he approached the outer wall of the moat. This was the nearly perpendicular counterscarp and he had an appalling time trying to make the ascent, with the dirt crumbling and sliding away under his hands and knees, and the bugle in his way, and with the Sepoys lined along the parapets behind him firing their muskets.

He hauled himself to the edge, the bullets drumming all around in the dirt, and he started blowing the advance. The bugle blared and blared in the smoky air, but still its shrill notes were lost in the tremendous din of battle.

Come on, Home prayed. *Why don't you come on?*

Colonel Campbell's waiting assault column was catching it from the storm of Sepoy fire. What had happened to Home and Salkeld? Why didn't the bugle blow? Suddenly everyone saw a thick pillar of smoke undulate beyond the corner that hid the Kashmir Gate. Was that the explosion? Campbell couldn't tell; the bellow of the British mortars right behind him drowned all other sound.

Wait—he thought he heard a bugle note!

"Enough of this waiting!" he roared. "We're going in!"

The 52nd Regiment, the Kumaon Gurkhas, and the 1st Punjab Infantry gave a mighty cheer and charged toward the red walls with fixed bayonets, running through the gunsmoke and shooting in extended order. Captain Crosse of the 52nd yelled at his friend Lieutenant Wilberforce:

"A guinea says I'm the first man in Delhi!"

He nearly didn't get it at all. The explosion had blown in only half of the gate and the passage was choked with smoking rubble. He and Wilberforce and a corporal named Taylor stopped by Carmichael's charred body and saw that the hole was just big enough to admit one man at a time. Grinning, his sword out, Crosse pushed by the other two and plunged through the shattered gate.

Wilberforce started to follow when the corporal

shoved him aside, saying, "After me, sir!" Wilberforce was the third man in.

The spearhead of the assault party pounded across
the wrecked drawbridge over the heads of Home's
huddled men. Inside the gate they found a reception
of dismembered Sepoy corpses, all killed by the explosion. They forced open the rest of the gate and
Campbell's entire column streamed into Delhi.

Six days later the vicious house-to-house street
fighting ended, and General Wilson gave Duncan
Home the honor of blowing open the last defense gate
in the Shah's palace. The Red Fort had fallen.

In the four months of fighting the British had suf-
fered 3,817 casualties: 992 killed, 2,795 wounded,
30 missing. Lieutenant Philip Salkeld was to be one
of the 992.

The sacrificial action that he and his comrades had
taken in blowing open the first gate was praised by
the entire British force. General Wilson said that
Salkeld would receive the Victoria Cross, hoping that
the news might give him strength and revive his will
to live. But Salkeld had no will left.

"It will be gratifying to send the medal home," he
murmured. He was awarded the V.C. posthumously.

The three English survivors of the explosion party,
Lieutenant Home, Sergeant Smith, and Bugler Hawthorne, also received the Victoria Cross. And the
wounded Sappers were awarded the Indian Order of
Merit and grants of land.

2 WOLFBOUND

The first time the two men noticed the wolf pack was just before the close of the short gray day. Gar Real heard the cry pierce the frozen tundra with a needlelike sharpness, and when he looked back the pack was grouped on a snow mound one-hundred yards behind them.

Gar shouted to Peter Ames who was running ahead of the lead dog, and they brought the team to a halt on the crisp, darkening snow. Ames knelt on the white field to get his breath. He had been breaking trail for two hours, running before the team and packing the new snow with his webbed snowshoes.

"Look back there, Peter," Gar called and pointed to the wolf pack. "Company," he added, and grinned.

Ames wiped a mittened hand across the bristly frost icicles clinging to his unshaven face and stared around at the frozen wasteland that surrounded them with white silence. His eyes went back to the distant pack and centered on a large gray wolf. There was a look of patient hunger on the wolf's face that touched the man with an obscure dread. He looked at Gar and saw him digging in the sled for their rifle.

"If you're going to risk a shot," he called, "try for that big gray. I reckon he's the leader."

Gar swung the rifle up with elaborate carelessness.

"One gray lobo—coming up!" he said.

The rifle cracked and a thin dun-colored wolf that stood at the big gray's flank tumbled into the snow with a high-pitched yelp. Instantly the rest of the pack turned on their fallen comrade with bared, tearing fangs.

"Butterfingers," Gar growled disgustedly and lowered the rifle. "Anyhow, that'll fill the rest of 'em for a while, eh?"

"It better," Ames murmured. "We've only got four shells left."

All around them the white world glimmered. The silence was complete now; the pack had pulled the dead wolf down the far side of the hill. The stillness was like electricity. Ames could sense it crackling on them. The wilderness stretched away to the encircling horizon of the lonely North.

Ames felt small and vulnerable in the magnitude of total nothingness. He looked back at the sled. Supplies low, ammo low, team fagged, and everywhere white winter hurrying in on them. And now. . . .

Somewhere behind them on the lost trail, beyond the last drifting mound, the call cracked the silence as a stone would crack glass. More timber wolves wailing their hunger against the wild.

Gar rocked the gee-pole from side to side to free the frozen runners.

"*Chook!*" he shouted at the resting team. The dogs struggled upward and threw themselves against the breast bands. The lead dog's bells began their merry tinkling; the harness creaked and the sled runners rasped across the frosted ground.

Out in the lead Ames plowed doggedly through the snow, cutting across the pale tableland that stretched endlessly, as if drawing them on inexorably. When he looked back he saw that the big gray had separated himself from the snarling wolves and was standing alone on the snowhill, watching the sled disappear into the wilds.

It was the winter of 1897, and from all over the globe thousands of gold-hungry men were flocking to the Yukon. A man had made a fabulous strike on the Klondike, and everyone from Jack London to Lime-juice Lil was stampeding across the treacherous icy trails to reach the glittering bonanza in the North.

By steamer, by raft, by pack train and dog sled, and on foot, they streamed across the great Canadian wilderness and the mighty Alaskan barrens. By sea and by river, through primordial forests and majestic rocky passes they toiled to reach the legendary El Dorado—always urged on and on by the magical words, "Gold strike in the Klondike!"

Peter Ames and Gar Real were young Canadian prospectors who had been panning a meager living along the foot of the Mackenzie River when the startling news of the great Klondike Strike had reached their eager ears. They had purchased an outfit and set out from Fort McPherson with the first snow, intending to follow the Porcupine River down to Fort Yukon, then take the Yukon to Dawson—the gold town that sat at the confluence of the Klondike and Yukon rivers.

But the snows had come early that winter and the cold wind off the Top of the World had rushed across Beaufort and Chuckchee Sea, over Brooks Range, and come at last to the twisting Porcupine.

Now Gar and Ames were running, not from the wolves, yet that was something to bear in mind, but from the white death surrounding them.

It was cold. The moist blast of the dogs' breath had settled on their furry faces like powder. Ames rubbed his cheeks to restore circulation. He thought it must be fifty below.

The gray day cast no shadow, for the sun was hidden behind a western mountain range. Knowing that night would soon be on them and that all travel must end, Ames studied the landscape. A spruce island veered south with a land drop running down the center. It was a tributary of the Porcupine—a frozen creek bed now, that made an easy trail.

"Gee ho!" he called, and the team labored down to the gray-white bed and through the low-growing spruce and came to a halt.

Silently the two men set up their small camp while the dogs sprawled out like dead things, but with their ears still perking at every movement beyond the glow of the fire. They could hear the wolves whining in the dark, restless in their hunger.

Ames looked up and saw two burning, slitted eyes

studying him. Slowly, the reflected eyes were joined by others and soon, wherever he looked, a pair of shining, hungry eyes stared back.

"They've slung a circle around us," he muttered. He reached for a flaming firebrand and with a quick snap sent it end-over-end into the circle of waiting wolves. The act was answered by a yelp and a scurry of movement, and the ring of eyes moved back a few yards and took up a new post.

"Don't," Gar said. "Our mutts are spooked enough already."

Ames looked at the husky team. They were on their feet by the fire now, whining and growling and bunching with nervous unrest.

"I wish they weren't such a green team," he said. "Think they know enough to sit tight?"

Gar grinned at him. "Wouldn't you?"

Ames said nothing. He crawled into his sleeping robe and cast a last worried glance at the icy blackness that shrouded their little glowing world of fire.

He awoke in the dark morning with the cry of the dog pack ringing in his ears. Gar was squatting before the fire pouring coffee. He turned to Ames and he spoke harshly.

"We got trouble."

Ames reached for his coffee, and said, "What?"

"Charlie's gone." Gar scowled into his cup. "The pack must have cut him out last night, somehow."

"They probably have a she-wolf running with 'em, and she drew Charlie out," Ames said. "We'll stake the mutts tonight."

Gar gave a sour grunt. "If we lose any more dogs, we'll be hauling that sled ourselves." Then, after a pause, he said, "I've never seen it, but I've heard tales that wolves will go for *more* than just the team dogs."

"It happens," Ames said, "if it's a hard winter, and if it's a big pack with a leader. Especially if it's a Canadian pack."

The luminous glow of the aurora borealis was passing slowly out of the dark sky. Dawn was still three hours distant. They hitched up the team and Gar on his snowshoes took the lead.

"*Chook!*" Ames cried, and the huskies lunged with tongues spilling out, and the sled runners began to move. As the sled shot off over the gray snow Ames looked back. And behind it followed the creatures of the wild—with equal determination.

The days of the winter Northland have little light and short duration. The two men could count on only seven hours of gray daylight, then they had to make camp. Gar fed the team their ration of frozen fish, and staked them to the ground for the night. He was approaching his plate of beans when the wolves' cry rang out.

"They ain't gonna give up," he said.

"No," Ames agreed. "Charlie just made a teaser for them. They're after the main course now."

In the night the wolves cut into the sleeping team.

Ames was shocked out of a troubled sleep by piercing cries that tore up the darkness. The silence was obliterated in a passion of savagery. He sat up and reached for a firebrand, staring into the dark bedlam of yelping, snarling, and snapping. Gar reached for the hand ax.

They rushed into the dark melee, Gar stumbling over a thrashing wolf, pausing to hack at the beast's head with the ax, the blood gushing out black on the gray snow, freezing instantly. Ames pitched two firebrands into the fray, and then swung at the white of snapping teeth with the third one, feeling the stick jar in his numb hand, and hearing the sound of the blow against skin-tight ribs.

And then, suddenly, there was only a high wailing howl as the wolf pack raced off into the savage land. Ames went back to the fire for another brand.

He stopped by the sled, staring and startled. There, not more than fifteen paces beyond the dying fire, the great gray wolf appeared.

The wolf's bright eyes sparkled with a penetrating look of mercilessness—and for a moment, Ames felt oddly hypnotized.

His eyes narrowed with hate, and he reached for the rifle. Instantly the two orbs of light winked out and the gray wolf was gone. *Gun-shy*, Ames thought. *An old hand.*

He joined Gar with a fresh firebrand, and waited for morning. Four dogs remained. The thin shaggy forms of three wolves lay dead on the snow.

"They got Kupi right here," Gar said. Then he pointed in the snow to a limp leather strap fastened to a short stake. It had been gnawed clean.

"That was Koko," he said. "They chewed his strap and cut him out."

Ames said nothing. He was thinking about the great gray wolf and of what he had said earlier: *It happens, if it's a big pack with a leader. . . .*

Into the dark frozen wild the two men fled. And behind them rose the cry of the pack. It soared with a rush and hung in the air until the highest note had been sounded, and then it fell back to the earth. To Ames, it was like a lost soul wailing in agony. He looked back and in the wan light saw the pack swing out in its usual half circle of pursuit.

One by one, he thought, and he shivered in his thick fur parka, and urged the fagging team on to greater speed.

At noon Gar stopped the team and trotted back to the sled, his snowshoes packing the smooth snow.

"I've had enough of this, Pete," he said, and reached for the rifle. "I'm gonna pick off that big gray lobo. With him gone, maybe the others will call it quits. Because if we don't shake that pack soon—we're dead."

Ames looked apprehensive. "It won't be easy, Gar. When that gray sees a rifle—he's gone!"

Gar grinned tightly through the glaze of his iced breath. "I'm no kid myself, Pete. I'm gonna bushwhack him." His eyes quickly skirted the desolate land.

"Tell you what. You pull the sled past that clump of spruce by that mound there. I'll drop off and wait for him, and you go on a ways like we was still running."

Ames shrugged and took the gee-pole in his mittened hand.

"All right. But watch yourself, Gar. There's something about that big gray mutt that—"

Gar jeered. "He's just a big timber wolf. I've shot dozens in my time. Now get along!"

The sled slid forward, and as it reached the clump of spruce Gar left Ames with a wink and disappeared around the snow mound. Ames moved the sled on for about three-hundred yards and then stopped in the middle of a vast snowfield. He paced up and down on his snowshoes and slapped his hands together to keep the numbness from them.

Half a dozen wolves suddenly appeared far back on the white ribbon of the sled track. When they saw the waiting sled, they stopped and started to mill about as if perplexed.

And then, from beyond the mound where Gar had hidden himself in ambush, the hungry cry rang shrill in the crystalline air. And the rifle cracked. Ames stood stock-still by the gee-pole and listened. Three more shots in rapid succession, and a loud outcry of snarling and yelping arose.

Ames grabbed the hand ax and started running across the crunching snow. "Gar!" he yelled. But when he had gone only one-hundred yards from the sled all sound from beyond the mound abruptly ceased and the deep white silence settled over the twilight land.

Ames slowed, stopped, stood uncertain in the middle of the empty field, the ax hanging heavily at his side. He knew without going any farther exactly what he would find beyond the mound, and the knowledge caught him in the stomach and threatened to make him sick. *Especially if it's a Canadian pack;* his own words repeated in his limp mind.

"Gar, Gar," he whispered.

He looked up past the clump of spruce to the snow-dusted ridge of the small hill. The great gray wolf was standing there alone, watching him with disappointed eyes.

In the few remaining hours of light Ames and the team raced against time, running toward the distant civilization of a trading post. Under the anticipation of a dreaded doom the four dogs and the man ran in silent desperation across the face of the winter world. But at the first warning of the coming night Ames swung the team into a small forest. There, with a high cliff at his back, he set up his small camp.

In the last minutes of dim light he set out to store up a large quantity of firewood against the night and the starved wolf pack. He was about sixty yards from the camp when he suddenly realized he had wandered too far in his search for wood. And worse—in his haste he had forgotten to unhitch the team!

A dozen slim, dark shadows separated themselves from the trees and, cutting wide around Ames, they ran through the woods and charged the husky team with sparkling eyes and bared fangs. The dogs bunched up and howled their anguish into the night, and then with a frantic bound they shot off through the woods, dragging the skittering sled behind them. At their heels, and in two long rows on either side, ran the pack in full cry.

The firewood tumbled from Ames' arms and he yelled after his dogs. But he knew he was wasting his breath. He would never see that team again. He picked up the wood and returned to the camp.

The high cliff offered him protection from the rear, and he placed his firewood in little piles to form a half circle out from the overhang. Within the space he piled his sleeping robe, the spare wood, his one pack of food, and built a cook-fire. He brewed his coffee, cooked his beans, and ate with the ax by his side.

As silently as drifting shadows the wolf pack slunk in and took their positions beyond the glare of the little sentry fires.

Through with his sparse meal, Ames checked his fires and moved back to the cliff. He sat down on the sleeping robe and studied the ring of hostile eyes.

"You got my team and my partner riding in your bellies," he muttered, "but you won't be content till you get me, will you? Well"—he picked up the ax and felt the thin edge of the blade—"you know where to find me."

It was a long hard night. He would doze for a bit, only to wake with a start to discover that the pack was edging in on him. Some of them had curled up in the snow and were in a restless sleep; others still squatted on their haunches and watched him with devouring eyes; and about seven of the more nervy ones had inched their gaunt bodies up to within springing distance.

Ames got to his feet hurriedly and scattered a handful of burning coals among them. With yelps and much snarling the shaggy brutes slunk back to a respectful distance and formed a new line. And within an hour it was all to be done over again.

The drab dawn showed Ames haggard and worn. But with the coming of morning the pack pulled farther back into the woods, and about half of them took off with their noses to the snow.

"That's right!" Ames yelled at them bitterly. "I'm a sure thing. I'll keep. But don't let any other game that might be running around loose get away from you!"

Wearily, he went out of camp and gathered a fresh supply of wood. The fire, he knew, was his only hope of survival. The ten or so remaining wolves became agitated by his movements and then skulked among the trees, whining and eyeing him with suspicion. He looked for the gray leader but could not find him among the gaunt guards.

He ate little that day, hoping to outstarve the pack. He knew that they would finally do one of two things: give him up and leave in search of easier prey, or—in the last moment of desperate hunger—rush him.

That night as they gathered around the camp the wolves pressed in to the point where some of them singed their fur on the fires. They seemed unusually nervous—snarling, whining, standing up, sitting down, moving backward, inching forward; and then Ames saw the reason for their unrest. The big gray was at their backs, growling a low persistent note into their peaked ears, pushing at them with his snout and snapping at their hindquarters, urging them to attack.

But the wolves weren't convinced. They trembled, whimpering, and some snapped back at the leader. The big gray was not discouraged. He kept at them, moving up and down the crouching line, agitating his followers into fury.

"That's right," Ames muttered, "egg 'em on. Get

'em to do your dirty work." He held the ax poised in his hand.

"What are you waiting for?" he yelled at them.

The wolves fell back a pace in alarm, and the big gray paused. With his ears perked, the gray wolf stared across the fire at the man with a look of rapt expectancy.

"You filthy cur!" Ames hissed. "Why don't you come on?"

The leader's eyes rested on the man for a moment longer. Then he licked his chops and turned back to his crouching companions. It went on like that for about fifteen minutes: the big gray doggedly prompting his mates to charge, and Ames holding them back with his curses. Until—

With a guttural growl, two of the wolves suddenly launched themselves over the flames at the man.

Ames' arm flung back and the ax blade flashed crimson in the firelight, and in a whistling arc it sliced out lip, teeth, and part of the first wolf's tongue. The wounded animal rolled wildly in the trampled snow as the second wolf swerved in confusion and backed into a fire, and then with a howl of pain and terror they were both leaping away in an orange-brown blur of fur and fire.

Far off through the crystal darkness Ames could hear the wounded wolf wailing his note of doom, and the answering cry of the pack that was close on him. And now there was only the man and the great gray wolf standing in the primeval wood with the little sentinel fires between them.

The wolf, with a look of consternation, turned and

stared into the covering night where his pack was pulling down their wounded comrade. Then, like a general who looks out on the battlefield and finds that his strategy has gone awry, the gray's eyes narrowed to two crafty pools of light, and with an air of indifference he curled up on the snow, doglike, and stared back at the man.

Within half an hour the ten remaining wolves returned and found their leader curled watchfully before the fires. With a great smacking of chops they took up their positions around the camp and settled down to wait out the night.

Ames watched them through heavy-lidded eyes. Time and again he caught his head nodding into a sleep that would be very final. After a while snow started to drift down through the branch-crossed air— not flaked, but delicate frost crystals. Slowly, Ames' leadened head began to nod, and. . . .

He awoke with a start to find himself within a shimmering ball of glassy sound. It was the hunger cry piercing through the frost on all sides of him. His fires had dwindled low and he could barely see the leering ring of wolfish faces.

He poked fresh wood into the waning fire piles, and pawed at his numb face in an effort to rub away the heavy woolly blanket of exhaustion that was wrapped around his brain.

The ring of grinning faces snarled and snapped at him, making short halting lunges, and he was forced into throwing some of the precious firebrands among them. But the pack only moved aside with a deft movement and let the brands sizzle out in the snow.

"So," he muttered, "you're not afraid of anything now, eh? You know I can't stay awake. You've run me down."

The intense eyes of the gray wolf caught his, and across the fire, the man and the beast built an invisible bridge of hate. The wolf's mouth opened, his pink tongue slipped out and little wells of saliva bubbled over his lower lip and made small holes in the snow at his feet. All the malignant evil of the ages seemed to glow in the leering face of this product of the timeless land.

He'll wait till I pass out, Ames thought. *Till it's impossible to defend myself, and then. . . .*

And then, in his dull despair, he became crafty. He sat down heavily with a weary sigh. His eyes fell shut, and opened. They shut again and after a longer pause, opened. Finally, they closed and his head nodded onto his chest. He grunted a low groaning noise and slowly lowered his head and shoulder into the snow.

The pack hunched up with open mouths and glittering eyes. The great gray gave a low warning snarl and the thick hair along the back of his neck bristled. His lips curled—and he sprang!

But Ames was watching the wolf through his heavy lashes, and his arm was tense and ready. As the gray body shot through the flames, the ax slashed through the air. The wolf screamed, and as Ames shoved up to meet him he bared his own teeth and screamed back at the blood-flecked face.

Then, with a hate that went beyond madness, he dropped the ax and grabbed the raging beast about its bloody, throbbing neck. Together they stumbled back to the cliff wall in a flurry of arms, claws, white teeth and fur, and in the firelight the glistening snow was dappled with icy crimson spots.

Suddenly Ames stopped struggling and looked at the mangled thing he held in his numb hands. The great gray wolf hung limp and still. He let the slashed body tumble to the snow and moved quickly to retrieve the ax. Standing poised and ready, he wondered why the rest of the pack held back.

"C'mon!" he bellowed at them. "What are you waiting for? Here I am! You want me to come out there?"

He cocked the ax over his shoulder and snatched up a firebrand and lumbered forward—a great fur-clad hulk of a man. He moved ahead three paces and stopped, glaring around crazily. The wolves drew hastily back from the fires and the raving man.

In blank bewilderment Ames watched the ten wolves gather under the snow-mantled trees. They whined and shuffled in the dark, rubbing against each other's shaggy hides and pausing to look inquiringly at the looming man and the circle of fire.

Silently, one by one they turned and slunk away into the dark frosted forest, leaving the man alone amidst his smoldering fires.

For a moment Ames was almost afraid to turn and look at the spot where he had dropped the dead wolf. He was half afraid that the big gray body wouldn't be there, that he had been caught up in something supernatural, or that his harassed mind had tricked him.

Quickly he turned around and looked toward the foot of the cliff. The lifeless form of the wolf lay there in a shaggy heap. Ames smiled and his body sagged with total fatigue. Wearily he stumbled over to his sleeping robe and fell on it.

Still smiling, he closed his eyes and went to sleep next to the body of the great gray wolf.

Two days later a group of Stick Indians out hunting game for their tribe, came upon a lone white man wandering dazedly along the frozen Porcupine. They took him to their camp and doctored him in their crude manner, and the following week they escorted him to Fort Yukon.

Peter Ames, like Jack London and most of the 30,000 hopeful prospectors who packed into the Yukon that winter, never did find any Klondike gold. But Ames, at least, had discovered something far more precious than gold—the value of a single human life.

3 BOLOS AT BALANGIGA

Day was dawning on the Philippine island of Samar when young Private Bertholf was relieved at his guard post near the bay of the little village of Balangiga. His relief guard grinned at him and said, "All's well, Bert?"

Bertholf grinned back. Everything was always All's Well in the isolated seaport village. . . .

It was Sunday morning, September 28, 1901. The Spanish-American War had been over for two years, and the United States had acquired the Philippine Islands as spoils of war. The U.S. Ninth Infantry was now busily engaged in occupying the multitude of large and small islands in a political policy known as "peaceful penetration."

A Philippine insurrectionist named Aguinaldo had bitterly fought the American penetration for nearly two years before he finally surrendered, and now there were only isolated incidents of native uprisings on the smaller outlying islands.

But nothing ever happened in peaceful little Balangiga.

One month before this fateful Sunday morning seventy-four men of C Company had arrived at Samar to occupy Balangiga. Looking at the jungle-locked village from the deck of the army transport ship *Ingalls*, Lieutenant Edward Bumpus had remarked to his men:

"Boys, we're in Googoo Land for sure, now. These natives are not our friends, but headhunters and savages."

But that had been a whole month ago, and the drowsy Samar days and somnolent nights had seemingly proven the lieutenant wrong. There had been no trouble in Balangiga.

"All's well and as right as rain," Bertholf said to his relief guard. "A few hours ago a whole batch of native women went into the church lugging some little coffins. I took a look in 'em. Seems they've had some kind of epidemic back in the bush and a lot of little kids died of it. They were just bringing the bodies in for services today. Well, I'm off for chow and some sack time."

Bertholf strolled back to the garrison, never dreaming that the "native women" were actually insurgent bolomen from the Samar jungle disguised in women's clothes, and that under each child's body in the little coffins (and one shudders to think how the savages had obtained these little corpses) were concealed sharpbladed bolos and barongs, the weapons of the Philippine insurgents. Now those bolomen were lurking inside the dark church, eagerly awaiting the word to attack.

It was to be an overwhelming massacre of the American troops, all carefully arranged by Pedro Abayan, the head man of Balangiga, and Pardo Sanchez, the village police chief.

For the past two days Sanchez had been bringing innocent-appearing bush natives into the garrison and setting them to work at chopping nipa palms for thatching roofs. Captain Thomas Connell, in command of the small garrison, had been completely taken in by Abayan's assumed friendliness and Sanchez' supposed helpfulness.

And why not? Nothing ever happened at Balangiga.

Private Bertholf strolled across the plaza past the church and convent (it was now officers' quarters), by the two-storied tribunal building (used as the main barracks), and climbed the bamboo steps to his squad hut to place his Krag rifle in the rack.

Coming down from the hut, which stood on eight-foot stilts like all the native quarters, he found the garrison coming to life. Soldiers were walking to the mess tents with their mess kits clattering in one hand while reading their letters from home in the other. Lieutenant Bumpus had returned from the fort at Basey only the night before, bringing along the mail and latest news.

Major Griswold, C Company's only medical officer, called from a convent window:

"Have you heard the news yet, Bertholf? President McKinley has been assassinated!"

Bertholf was stunned. Nothing as outrageous as that had happened in America for thirty-six years! Shaking his head in amazement, he entered the kitchen. Sergeant Markley and two privates from his squad, Allen and Degraffenreid, were sitting at the table waiting for Cook Melvin Walls to feed them.

"Can a hungry man get a bite here?" Bertholf asked. "I'm just off guard duty and want to grab some sleep."

"Sit ye down, Berty me boy," Sergeant Markley said. "Walls will sling ye up a nice mess of hash. Heard the bad news?"

Bertholf nodded and sat down. Glancing out the open window, he saw Police Chief Sanchez herding his native workmen across the plaza. There were eighty of them, but neither Bertholf nor anyone else gave them a moment's thought.

Aside from the eighty natives chopping nipa with their keen-edged bolos, there were more than twenty armed natives waiting in the church. And just beyond the boundaries of the garrison, there were three hundred bolomen hiding in the bush.

Sanchez glanced around with a satisfied eye. The Americans had only four armed men posted on guard duty, and he had dozens of concealed bolomen ready to pounce on each one of them when he gave his signal.

Sanchez smiled warmly at First Sergeant Randalls who was walking to the water barrel to wash his mess kit, and then strolled on over to Sergeant Betron's hut where Betron and Corporal Burke and the six men of their squad were eating in the blue shade under their quarters.

The police chief leaned against one of the support posts, and Corporal Burke came out to talk to him about McKinley's assassination. Sanchez pretended to be deeply grieved.

Private Gamlin had just finished his breakfast and was hurrying by the huts to relieve the sentinel on Number Two post. He was carrying his Krag over his shoulder. As he passed Sanchez and Burke, the police chief suddenly stopped talking and took two or three fast steps after him.

Without warning, Sanchez snatched Gamlin's rifle from him by the barrel and swung the butt against the startled soldier's head, killing him on the spot. Sanchez immediately let out a mighty yell and instant pandemonium broke loose over Balangiga!

The church bell began to clang and dozens of conch shells wailed from the jungle hills. With a crash the huge church doors flew open and out poured the hidden natives, yelling like demons, to join the eighty "workmen" who were already slashing at the surprised soldiers with bolos, barongs, picks, and shovels.

Caught off-guard in separated groups of four or five or even less, and armed with only their knives and forks and mess kits, the Americans did not stand a prayer of a chance.

The three hundred bolomen burst out of the bush and simply overwhelmed the four stunned sentries— hacking and chopping them to red ribbons. Screaming like demented banshees they swept across the plaza and into the convent, the tribunal, the kitchen, and the squad huts.

Corporal Burke, recovering from his gape-mouthed amazement, sprang on Sanchez just as the Filipino tried to bring up Gamlin's rifle. Both men wrestled their way into the hut.

A bloody melee took place in Betron's hut, with dozens of howling bolomen piling in through the open rattan walls. Private Clark lost an arm with one deft slash of a bolo, and the blood spurting from his stump bathed the floor red. Private Driscoll tried to crawl out the door on hands and knees, his split skull dripping. Sergeant Betron's slashed and bleeding squad fought a desperate hand-to-hand fight for possession of the rifle rack.

Burke hit the floor with Sanchez and two other bolomen on top of him and, though certain that he was a goner, he struggled like a madman to shake off his assailants. One of his outflung hands encountered a revolver on the floor and he started firing from flat on his back, blasting off Sanchez and the other two.

The surprise attack was so sudden that First Sergeant Randalls never even saw it coming. One of the native workmen split his skull with an ax as the sergeant was bending over the water barrel washing his mess gear.

A horde of bolomen ganged up on the mess tents and slashed the guy ropes, dropping the heavy Sibley tents on top of the scrambling soldiers. Then they started hacking at the struggling men caught under the bloody canvas, their bolos rising and falling, rising and falling. . . .

Sergeant John Closson, a giant of a soldier, came bellowing and laying about like an enraged bull from under one of the collapsed tents. He led a handful of frantic soldiers in a wild rush up the bamboo steps to the upper floor of the tribunal where their rifles were racked.

The howling bolomen went with them, slashing and clawing at their backs. The bamboo steps splintered under the tremendous weight of the struggling men and collapsed in a great thrashing of arms and legs and knives.

By ones and twos, soldiers who had escaped from the mess tents fought like fury with nothing but their mess gear for weapons, flaying out right and left in a desperate attempt to ward off the attackers.

A raving tide of bolomen swept into the convent and caught Lieutenant Bumpus still in bed, and he was butchered in his army blankets without a chance to defend himself.

Major Griswold tried to escape down the back stairs to the church and was hacked to pieces on the steps.

Captain Connell rolled out of bed as the blood-crazed bolomen burst into his room and managed to defend himself with his sword long enough to back up to his open window. Spinning about, he leaped through the window and landed all a-sprawl in the plaza below. Gaining his feet, he started to run toward the sound of gunfire (Sergeant Betron's hut) when he was mobbed by yelling natives only twenty feet from the convent and killed.

The massacre at Balangiga was now only two minutes old and already some thirty American soldiers were dead or dying. At this tense moment it looked as though C Company was about to be annihilated without one spark of resistance.

When the church bells first started to clang, Cook Walls had been dishing out hash to Sergeant Markley and the three privates. Then the ear-splitting yelling of the charging bolomen had wailed across the plaza, and at that moment some soldier outside the kitchen had cried:

"The Googoos are in on us! Run for your lives!"

Almost at once four insurgent Filipinos jammed up in the kitchen door and made the air bright with their flashing bolos. One of them broke loose and darted around the table to take a swing at Sergeant Markley's head.

Markley, a bearlike man, sprang to his feet and threw his plate of hash into the native's distorted face; and Bertholf—acting on impulse—spun on the bench and jabbed his fork into the boloman's exposed midriff. The Filipino doubled over in screaming pain as Markley bellowed:

"Get to your rifles, boys!"

Suiting the action to his words, he pile-dived through the other bolomen—kicking, straight-arming, shouldering his way out of the kitchen. Covering ground in a broken run, he dodged through and plunged into his squad hut and snatched up a rifle and bullets.

As he stepped up to the front window, he spotted Corporal Arnold Irish who was in the midst of a terrifying nightmare only fifteen feet away.

Irish had darted out of one of the mess tents the moment after the attack. Caught in the open plaza alone and unarmed, he had run an erratic path through a dozen or more bolo-swinging savages, almost reaching his squad hut when a native policemen clobbered him with a club.

The policeman was just about to hit him again when Markley killed him with his rifle. Stunned and bleeding, Corporal Irish rose to his feet and stumbled into his hut to get his rifle. A moment later he ran across the open ground and joined Markley, and with him came Private Swanson with a Krag in his hands.

Now, three minutes after the initial onrush of bolomen, little isolated pockets of American resistance began to form.

In Sergeant Betron's hut, Betron, Burke, Privates Armani and Gibbs—all slashed by bolos—won the fight over the rifle rack and drove the bolomen through the windows and doors. With rapid fire they commenced to scare the insurgents to cover.

"Listen!" Betron commanded his comrades. "They're firing from Markley's hut. C'mon—let's join 'em!"

The four wounded soldiers rushed into the open and ran toward Markley's besieged hut. Until that moment Corporal Irish had thought that he and Markley and Swanson were the only survivors of the entire Balangiga garrison.

But there were others. Scattered and alone, they were fighting in a way that few men had ever fought before.

When Markley made his mad dash from the kitchen Bertholf sprang to his feet and started to follow him— only to be attacked by two fanatical bolomen.

Flaying and hammering at the savages with his mess kit—his only weapon—Bertholf was just about to be slaughtered when the cook pitched a boiling pot of coffee at the savages.

Melvin Walls began to throw canned goods, and then snatched up a meat cleaver and charged through the door with Bertholf, Allen, and Degraffenreid right at his back. Running into the open and looking wildly around for cover or weapons, Bertholf spotted a nearby rock pile.

"Here we go, boys!" he yelled, and led the way up to the top of the pile.

Instantly the four soldiers found themselves besieged by a swarm of bolomen who tried to climb the pile from every side. The soldiers held them off by pitching rocks at them with both hands—but they couldn't hope to hold out for long.

A glinting bolo hit Walls, who rolled down the rocky slope, leaving a trail of blood behind him.

"Rocks ain't good enough!" Bertholf yelled. "Run for the main barracks and get the rifles."

Not pausing to see if his buddies were with him, Bertholf took a springing leap from the top of the rock pile, flying right over the gawking head of a crouching boloman, hit the ground with a thud, and was off for the barracks.

He didn't know it, but he was running straight into the most savage fighting in Balangiga.

Sergeant Closson, the giant of the garrison, was one of the few infantrymen who reached the upper story of the tribunal before the bamboo stairs collapsed. He and the remaining men of his squad were immediately set upon by a gang of bolomen who had come thundering up the back stairs.

The Yankess fought through the rooms with their knives and mess kits, a pick or bolo one of them had snatched from a native, and even a baseball bat that had suddenly appeared from nowhere. It was a masterful struggle, and by the time Bertholf and his comrades were reaching the rock pile, the bodies of the combatants in the tribunal were piled three deep.

And suddenly Closson found himself all alone in a room filled with yowling bolomen. . . .

Bare-handed, his back to a blood-splattered wall, Closson fought them off with his fists, feet, knees, and the butt of his head. But they kept coming at him like a hungry school of sharks—hacking and thrusting and lunging, and screaming, always screaming.

His muscular arms were crisscrossed with bolo cuts; a barong slashed his scalp; he was hammered and hacked and driven to his knees . . . and then with his bull-like roar he shoved to his feet and smashed the jaw of a savage with his huge fist, grabbed the man's rifle and cartridge belt and, pivoting about, took a running leap out of the nearest window.

He came down hard, but got to his feet immediately and started loading the rifle from the bandolier, limped around the corner to the front of the building, and bowled over three running bolomen with the rifle as he went. When he reached the front door of the tribunal he met Privates Considine, Manire, and Bertholf.

When Bertholf raced away from the rock pile, he had dodged around the front of the kitchen and slammed right into none other than Pedro Abayan, the head man of Balangiga—who had a Colt pistol in his hand and used it quickly.

But he fired from the hip, and the slug went wide. Bertholf had a rock clenched in his right hand. He brought it down on Abayan's skull. Snatching up the Colt, he started for the tribunal again. There he came upon Considine and Manire. They had a shovel and a spade and were hammering at a handful of natives who were holding the doorway.

Bertholf started to blast the insurgents aside with the Colt just as Closson came limping up to them. Closson also shot into the pack and the insurgents fell aside in disorder. Manire and Considine picked up a couple of rifles and the four soldiers forced their way into the hall.

Through the cracks in the rattan wall of the orderly room, they saw a milling mob of natives on whom they opened fire at point-blank range.

"All right, boys," Closson said. "Let's clear the plaza!"

Meanwhile, Betron, Markley, Burke, Irish, and three or four more had joined at Markley's hut and were putting up a stiff fight with their Krags. But Betron— now the senior noncom in command—knew that their position was untenable. They couldn't possibly hold the hut against three-hundred or more bolomen.

"Fall back and rally at the flagpole in the plaza!" he ordered.

The little group of desperate soldiers broke out of the hut and ran toward the flagpole where Old Glory flew at half-mast in memory of the President. There they were joined by Corporal Hickman and Privates Allen and Degraffenreid, who had fought their way clear of the rock pile.

A few minutes later Closson, Bertholf, Considine,

and Manire trotted across the corpse-littered plaza and fell in with the hard-pressed American soldiers who were about to make their last stand beneath the flag of the United States.

Sergeant Betron looked around at his little cluster of bleeding men. Nearly every one of them had been slashed one or more times, and some were very near death.

"I ain't no General Custer, to be slaughtered like a hog in the open!" he roared. "Form up—every man who can lift a Krag!"

A dozen grim-faced Yankees formed three squads of four men each, and they spearheaded down the three main streets of Balangiga, driving the bolomen back into the jungle by the determined impetus of their charge. At Betron's order, they fell back to the flagpole and braced themselves for the next attack.

For one long hour the Americans held their position in the plaza while the enemy milled on the outskirts of Balangiga but did not advance. Betron called the roll and only thirty-six of C Company's men answered. Nineteen of these were so badly wounded they could not even load their weapons, and twelve others were classified as "walking wounded." That left five able-bodied soldiers.

The battle, as far as the insurrectionists were concerned, was far from over. The conch shells continued to blow in the jungle and more and more bolomen were gathering around Balangiga.

"We're closed in by land," Betron said to Sergeants Markley and Closson. "So we'll have to attempt a retreat by water. Let's git!"

On Balangiga's muddy shore they found two large native boats, called barotas, and three small boats. Betron put twelve men in one barota, thirteen in the other, and divided the remaining eleven among the three smaller vessels.

"Markley," Betron said, "you and Swanson take one of the little barotas and go on ahead to Basey to report and fetch us help."

Markley hesitated, staring back at the village.

"Wait a minute," he said. "We've forgotten the flag. Who'll risk his carcass with me to bring out the old girl?"

"Me," Bertholf said, and a Private Wingo said, "Me too, Sarge."

Strung out in a line the three men ran back into Balangiga, across the blood-soaked plaza and up to the flagpole, with insurgent rifles shooting at them from the shadowy jungle and the surrounding huts.

Wingo reached the flagstaff first and hauled down the colors, as Markley and Bertholf covered him with rapid rifle fire. The plaza rang with bullets as Markley yelled, "Let's git out of here, boys!"

Triumphantly, the three soldiers carried Old Glory down to the shore.

With the wounded lying every which way in the crowded boats, the little fleet shoved off. The savages came screaming out of the jungle to stop them, but the few soldiers who could still lift a rifle scattered them with a volley. Markley and Swanson went on ahead out of the bay. It was going to be a long, hard, twenty-mile haul to Basey.

Bertholf, miraculously unwounded, was in com-

mand of one of the small barotas. He had Privates
Marak, Armani, and Buhrer with him, all severely
wounded. Marak could help a little with a clumsy pad-
dle. The other two were helpless. Bertholf's boat was
about a hundred yards ahead of the third small barota,
which contained Privates Wingo, Powers, and Driscoll
(how Driscoll managed to crawl out of Balangiga and
down to the boats with his skull split open is a mystery).

Bertholf looked back and saw that Wingo's boat
was in trouble. In skirting the headland they had
struck the rocks, and now their craft was swamping
in the surf. A mob of savages burst from the jungle to
cut them down. Powers took off through the shallows
to try to make a break into the bush. Wingo, the man
who had saved Old Glory, now tried to save Driscoll.
They were both butchered in their swamped boat.

The beleaguered boats crawled slowly up the coast,
followed by sharks that were attracted by the blood
dripping from the wounded. Every so often a group
of insurgents would put out from the shore in barotas
to give chase, but rifle fire held them off.

And now Bertholf's boat was in trouble. Marak
called excitedly from the bows. "Bert! This tub is leak-
ing like a sieve!"

It was indeed. The hull of the little barota was as
rotten as old Swiss cheese, and in another minute
they would be foundering. Bertholf looked around at
the nearby jungle. No savages were in sight at the
moment, so he turned the waterlogged craft in to shore.

With Marak's help, Bertholf managed to get the
wounded and dazed Armani and Buhrer out of the
boat and into the jungle. They found a little hollow

among some downed nipa palms and sprawled out on the sand. Bertholf tried to do what he could for his wounded companions, but without even a first aid kit it wasn't much.

"The swine!" Marak hissed furiously. "The filthy swine!"

"Shut up!" Bertholf whispered. "Likely there are Googoos all through the bush looking for us."

Through the sweltering afternoon they lay in their shelter, apprehensively looking at the surrounding jungle. Then it was night.

"There's a little fisherman's village about a mile up the coast," Bertholf said. "I'm gonna slip in there and see if I can swipe a barota. You stay here with Armani and Buhrer."

"No," Marak said. "I'll go nuts if I sit here any longer waiting to be butchered. I'm coming with you."

The moon was showing over the tops of the scrub bushes now, white and full. Bertholf and Marak moved through the jungle by the feel of the ground underfoot, like panthers, and as silently. Marak was sweating, and was thankful when Bertholf cautioned him to stop.

The jungle ended like a sudden wall. There was no gradual merging of trees into the little fishing village. A wall of timber stood like an irregular palisade around a small shallow lagoon. A flotilla of barotas was drawn up on the moonlit shore.

Bertholf and Marak slipped from the trees, across the beach, and shoved off in a fifteen-foot barota. No one saw them come or go. The village slumbered on. Within half an hour the two desperate men were paddling down the coast to the spot where they had left their swamped barota.

"Oh, Lord!" Marak hissed. "Look!"

A dazzle of flaming torches illuminated a pocket of the jungle in the black shore. Then they heard the wild yelling. The savages had found Armani and Buhrer!

Crouching down to the gunwales of their craft, the two men stared bleakly at the scene being enacted in the jungle. Then, wordlessly, they turned their barota around and started paddling north.

Sergeant Markley and Swanson had lost their course in the night and had accidentally crossed the channel and landed on the island of Leyte, where they made their way to the army post at Tanauan.

Sergeant Betron arrived at Basey with the two large barotas at four A.M. He had brought in twenty-five men, twenty-two of them badly wounded. Two others had died of wounds en route. Nine of them would die later in the Basey hospital. Bleeding, sunburnt, blistered by insect bites, many of them retching and half out of their minds from having drunk saltwater when their water supply gave out at noon the day before, the battered survivors of Balangiga were carried from the barotas.

Sergeant Markley, Corporal Hickman, and Corporal Irish were the only men able to stand on their own feet. At nine A.M. Captain Edwin Bookmiller left Basey with fifty-five men from G Company to return to Balangiga on the steamship *Pittsburg*. Corporal Irish accompanied them.

Just about this time Bertholf and Marak were toiling up the coast in their stolen barota, when they spotted a khaki-clad figure lying on the Samar shore. It was Private Powers, and how he had managed to travel that far on foot, alone and unaided and wounded, nobody would ever know. He was dead when Bertholf and Marak reached him.

At ten A.M. the *Pittsburg* picked up the two weary privates at sea. Marak was turned over to the surgeon, and Bertholf went below with Irish to eat and drink.

At twelve-thirty P.M. the *Pittsburg* put in to Balangiga Bay. The savages had set the tribunal afire, and a great howling mob of bolomen rushed down to the shore to meet the landing troops. A Gatling gun on the steamer's deck sent an angry burst of lead across the beach and the insurgents scattered in a panic.

Bertholf and Irish scrambled into one of the landing boats and came ashore with the Ninth Infantry. Charging with fixed bayonets the fifty-eight soldiers fanned through Balangiga with rebel yells and cowboy yells. The bolomen fled into the jungle in a hysteria of fear, and it was a quick victory for the Americans. But there was no cheering.

Grimly the men of G Company looked at the carnage that littered the plaza. The bodies of the thirty-six slain soldiers had been mutilated beyond description.

The honorable dead were given a military funeral in a mass grave in front of the church. Bertholf and Irish accompanied Captain Bookmiller as he made a hurried count of the enemy dead for his report.

At least those of us who went down under the bolos of the savages made a good account of ourselves, Bertholf thought. For the bolomen had paid dearly for the thirty-six dead Americans. Bookmiller estimated that more than two-hundred and fifty Filipinos had been killed in the massacre.

Colonel E. G. Peyton, USA, who later wrote on Balangiga, said: "That almost forgotten fight in that faraway Philippines really deserves a place in history alongside Thermopylae, Balaclava, the Alamo and the Little Big Horn."

4 THE GREAT TOUH

A Black Cape buffalo, the most cunning and ferocious animal in Africa, followed a game track around a small hill and wandered into the Fort Archambault territory on the Chari River. Encountering two Djinge natives who were out hunting, the great beast was instantly all fire and fury, and, lowering his massive head, he charged. The two bushmen only escaped him by swimming the river.

Within the hour the entire Djinge village was cowering inside their mud-and-wattle huts in fear of the roving buffalo.

Captain Armand Brigaud was in command of the district in the South Chad territory of what at the time was French Equatorial Africa. He knew that something would have to be done about the buffalo. But he also knew that it was a very serious business for a nonprofessional hunter to try to track and shoot an African buffalo, and there were no professional hunters in Fort Archambault. Besides himself, there were only four French sergeants and a doctor named Ramme.

However, one of the sergeants, a man named Berthaud, was highly enthusiastic about becoming a big game hunter. He was absolutely certain that he could kill the buffalo.

"Let me have a crack at him, sir. I'll bring the *sacré* beast down as easily as I would a hog. All one needs is a heavy-bore rifle, a good eye, and a steady hand."

"Why don't you let him try it," Doctor Ramme suggested to Bigaud at the mess table, "since you haven't the stomach for the job yourself?"

The doctor and the captain did not get on well at all. Ramme was obsessed with bug collecting and he "borrowed" all the alcohol in the infirmary to use for pickling his insects, and Brigaud was of course always objecting to this high-handed acquisition of medical supplies.

But the truth was, Ramme had been right. Brigaud didn't have the stomach to face a Black Cape buffalo; nor did he care to risk the life of any man in his command on such a dangerous undertaking.

"No, Sergeant. It's out of the question. Much too risky."

But Berthaud refused to take no for an answer. For two days he pestered the captain for permission to hunt down the buffalo, and finally, with misgiving, Brigaud gave in to the persistent soldier.

"Very well. But whether you kill him or not—be back here by tomorrow noon, not a minute later. That's a direct order."

"Certainly. Have no fear, Captain. The job is as good as done!" Berthaud assured his officer, and he set out happily with a Massa gunbearer and a Djinge guide, tramping away with all the confidence of a great white hunter.

Berthaud did not return the following day, nor did the guide or the gunbearer. Fearing the worst, Brigaud sent out a search patrol, and they found what was left of the sergeant. It was a ghastly sight. The buffalo had trampled and gored the soldier's body until it was almost unrecognizable. Hearing the grim news, Brigaud went out to inspect the grisly evidence.

Two cartridges had been fired from Berthaud's rifle, and there were congealed blood splotches on the grass forty feet away from the body. Evidently Berthaud had wounded the buffalo with at least one shot, and then, enraged in a way that only a Black Caper can become, the brute had charged him.

Other evidence indicated that the horrified gunbearer and guide had instantly dropped their weapons and fled into the bush, leaving the luckless sergeant to face the savage onrush alone. Sadly, the patrol party carried Berthaud's remains back to the fort.

The frightening news spread rapidly throughout the area. A white soldier had been killed by a giant bull buffalo; bullets could not stop the monster; surely, the Djinge and Massa tribesmen of the neighborhood reasoned, the great beast was endowed with supernatural powers. True, the French captain might be in command, but the buffalo ruled the territory! And, out of the fantastic scare-legends they created around him, they gave the buffalo a name: The Great Touh.

It was with a rather empty feeling in the pit of his stomach that Brigaud quickly came to realize that all the neighboring bushmen were starting to look down on him. What was far worse, his own African soldiers obviously felt the same. He had greatly fallen in everyone's esteem, and if he did not soon do something about Touh he would lose face.

The final straw came when the irate doctor suddenly turned on him. Some containers of alcohol had arrived by steamboat up the river, and Brigaud had promptly locked up every bottle of it before Ramme could use it to preserve the bugs he collected.

"I think you are a poor sport, Captain," Ramme said. "You know that everybody expects you to avenge Berthaud's death by ridding the community of Touh; yet you sit here and do nothing."

Now it was a question of honor. Without a word, Brigaud walked to the rifle rack, selected Berthaud's hunting rifle, and went outside, calling for two native soldiers and a Djinge trapper named Bopa.

Bopa, nosing the ground like a fox hound, led the way through a few Massa huts. Soon they left every sign of human habitation behind. The track wandered on through belts of silver-gray trees growing out of the bare sand and spreading aloft gnarled branches of brown leaves against the sky.

There was neither sound nor movement around them as the little group trekked across a wilderness of sand and withered trees. It went on like this for three days, and it was in the late afternoon of the third day when they reached a rippling sea of swale grass. Bopa, still intently studying the track that was totally in-comprehensible to Brigaud, led them toward a thicket of thin reeds and tall, wavering grass.

Bopa went down on one knee, holding his spear like an antenna, to study the track. Then he pointed to the thicket, and Brigaud nodded. The last thing on earth Brigaud wanted to do was to go into that mysterious thicket. A Black Cape buffalo was bad enough, but a wounded one in a dense thicket was a living horror on hooves. Yet it had to be done.

The thicket was like a green wall, ten feet high. They followed a little passageway the buffalo must have made. They started into it—Bopa pushing ahead, stepping cautiously, then Brigaud with Berthaud's rifle, and finally the two native soldiers with Lebel rifles.

The reeds kept whipping back in his face, powdering him with dust. The air was acrid, and the reeds getting thicker, taller. The passageway was becoming a tunnel, and other tunnels began to cross their passage. Bopa seemed to be lost. He paused in bewilderment.

Bopa located the track again and they pushed forward into the reeds. Suddenly something took off overhead with a wild fluttering noise and Brigaud jumped nervously. Bopa was cowering before him, his muddy eyes big with fright and angling up and over his shoulder, gawking at the green roof above.

"Buffalo birds," Brigaud murmured. "Go on, Bopa."

He was trying to recall the vague information he had once heard about Cape buffalos. You were never supposed to shoot at a buffalo's head because the horn-base of his thick skull was as hard as a steel helmet. The buffalo always charged with his neck and head straight out, and you were supposed to hit him on the point of his muzzle or squarely in the chest.

Brigaud had a vivid mental picture of the great Touh charging him as he tried to hold a shaky bead on the huge beast's broad wet muzzle, and a trill of nervous fear went up his spine.

Abruptly the tunnel opened like a cave's mouth, and the four men filed into a passageway where they could stand up straight. Overhead they could see a few traces of turquoise sky. That made Brigaud feel much better.

Bopa was contemplating the track again. He had three green forks to choose from. From where Brigaud stood they all appeared to run into blind alleys. Bopa mumbled something to himself and pointed straight ahead.

Brigaud started to follow the guide, when his foot snagged in a root, and for a split second he was all flailing arms as he tried to keep himself from falling and making a crashing noise. One of the native soldiers caught him by the arm and supported him till he recovered his balance. But Bopa wasn't aware of the holdup, and it gave him time to work himself some yards ahead of the others.

Brigaud looked forward and saw the Djinge guide step through a loose screen of undulating grass . . . and right then they all heard the deep-chested snort of a buffalo.

Brigaud stopped in his tracks, and the first native

soldier bumped into his back. There was a rush of movement and a scream that instantly destroyed Brigaud's equilibrium. Then there was a sharp sound and he knew that death was coming like a flying wedge, and out of the green reeds hurtled Bopa!

The guide was coming head over heels, helplessly, and something seemingly as large and powerful as a locomotive was thundering after him. Brigaud whipped up his rifle and fired blind, but the shot clicked on a defective cartridge. At the same instant both African soldiers leaped headfirst into the thicket, even as Brigaud shouted, "Fire, you fools!"

Then he saw the outstretched square head, the slick, glistening, silver muzzle, the great, low-slung, bat ears, the black horns. And all of it was coming at him!

Something happened to Brigaud. He threw himself at the thicket in a blind fury of smashing, plowing, boot-lashing insanity. The noise was all rolled into a ball around him—the smash of the thicket, the bellow of the Cape buffalo, and the soldiers screaming. And Brigaud knew he was adding to the panic, but he couldn't stop himself. He simply had to get out of there.

The instinct of self-preservation had awakened in him. Crashing, lunging along, falling and crawling on the ground, he approached the edge of the thicket.

He paused, gasping for his breath, looking around, listening. The Cape buffalo snorted furiously somewhere nearby, and Brigaud leaped up and broke out of the thicket.

Both of the frenzied soldiers were ahead of him. They had dropped their rifles and were racing for a nearby mopani tree. Brigaud threw a glance over his shoulder and saw the outraged buffalo barging from the thicket close behind him. He didn't waste any time scooting for a mopani himself.

He jumped, grabbed a lower limb, the soles of his boots scrabbling frantically at the rough bark as the huge horned head of the Cape buffalo slammed the trunk only inches below his heels. The shocking impact rattled the little tree so violently that Brigaud was almost pitched out of the whipping branches.

Touh backed off for another charge, and Brigaud hurriedly climbed higher—which was not actually very high, because the mopani is a small, stunted tree. He wedged himself into an uncomfortable fork as Touh rammed his massive head into the trunk again. The vibration jarred Brigaud's trembling body, and the branches thrashed as if in a spasm, raining a great flutter of leaves and twigs.

Touh circled the tree, pausing to paw at the grass and snort. Every so often he would lunge forward and hammer at the trunk. Trembling in his low perch, Brigaud stared down at the formidable beast; squat, barrel-bodied, bluish-black, nearly hairless, with great curling black horns, Touh bore the fearsome aspect of the world's most dangerous game.

Watching him, Brigaud suddenly sensed the loss of something he had always unconsciously held as invulnerable. He had lost his courage. He was like a cringing, frightened monkey cowering in a tree, unable to help himself in any manner.

What could be done? Help was eight miles away, and the three sergeants probably wouldn't send out a patrol for another two days. When they did, they

would probably try to follow Brigaud's old trail—
which would start them out in the wrong direction!
It might take them three more days to track him down!
Three to five days stuck in a tree without food or
water in the blistering African heat. Nor was there
much hope that Touh would tire of the game and go
away.

Brigaud cranked around in his tight fork and looked
to the west. The glow of sunset was touching the crests
of far-off stone hills with orange and flooding the sea
of swale grass and mopanis with purple. Soon the hills
loomed up in black masses around the horizon, screen-
ing the lower stars.

Night. Brigaud was tired, very hungry, and madden-
ingly thirsty. It grew cold. Then, to make matters
worse, a colony of big black ants found him. Their
burning stings kept him squirming and scratching and
slapping at himself. He could hear the two soldiers
groaning in the dark. They must have been having
the same problems in their tree.

Sleep was impossible. The ants were bad enough,
but every so often Touh would take a running charge
at Brigaud's mopani and nearly rattle him from his
perch.

In the first pale suggestion of dawn, Brigaud, haggard and gaunt and still perched in his tree like a tired
owl, turned his face to the east and muttered, "Come
on! Come on, dawn!"

When it grew light, Brigaud looked down. Touh
was still there.

A metallic glint in the swale grass caught Brigaud's

eye, and he saw that one of the rifles which the soldiers had dropped was midway between their tree and the thicket. Sixty feet distant.

He would have to get to that rifle somehow.

He shouted to the two soldiers: "Begin cursing and howling at Touh!"

"But why, Captain?" one of them called back.

"To take his mind off me for a while! See if you can distract his attention."

The two understood and they immediately set up a shrill outcry. Touh's batwing ears flapped and he snorted explosively, instantly inflamed with anger. Seemingly he had forgotten all about the soldiers until that moment. He bolted forward.

His horns, which had a three-foot spread, thundered into the tree trunk and the two terrified soldiers hung on for dear life. Aside from the fact that there were two of them cramped together up there, their mopani was even smaller than Brigaud's. They were in very real danger as Touh slammed his massive head against the trunk.

They screamed in terror. Brigaud knew he was going to have to do something quickly. He started releasing his tortured body from its painful perch, got a two-handed grip on an arm-thick branch, and prepared to swing himself down to the turf.

He stalled, watching the enraged Touh—waiting until the buffalo swung his hindquarters around, thinking he might stand a chance to reach the rifle when Touh's back was turned.

All at once the Cape buffalo seemed to lose interest.

He swung his big head away and ambled off a dozen feet, lifting his damp muzzle toward the climbing sun. His back was to Brigaud.

"Now's my chance!" he thought.

He swung down on the branch and dropped heavily to the ground. But his muscle-cramped legs wouldn't support his weight and he crumpled to both knees with an agonized gasp.

Touh reared around with amazing agility and started making a furrowing course through the grass, running straight for Brigaud. Cunning was the right word for the Cape buffalo!

Brigaud spun about, took three fast hobbling steps back to his mopani, and scrambled up into the high branches while Touh hammered on the trunk like a powerful battering ram.

At noon Touh resumed his attack on the other tree, battering the splintered trunk again and again. The two soldiers howled piteously as the elastic branches whipped and plunged and snapped back. Surely, Brigaud thought desperately, one of them would soon fall out.

Brigaud slid down to the ground, yelling. Touh charged him, and he scampered up his mopani again. It went on that way for two exhausting hours until Brigaud no longer had the strength to make another climb. He slumped in his tree, gasping for breath. Touh returned to the other tree.

A stranger suddenly appeared, another, smaller bull. Touh's eyes rolled furiously and he let out a tremendous bellow. Lowering his enormous head, he launched himself at the startled newcomer.

Brigaud hastily tumbled out of his tree and raced across the swale to snatch up the rifle. All the exercise that Touh had put him through had been of some use; it had limbered up his stiffened joints and muscles.

He checked to see that the rifle was loaded and ready. Then he looked for Touh. The Cape buffalo had chased the smaller bull back into the thicket, and now was wheeling around. Then he spotted Brigaud standing alone on the open ground.

In that instant something seemed to break inside Brigaud. For a moment he thought he was going to drop the rifle and run for the tree again. But he didn't. He stood his ground, braced and ready for the charge. He thought of Berthaud and of Bopa, and raised the rifle.

And then he was all right. Even as Touh's head stretched out and his driving hooves got under way with a back kick of dirt and weed, he felt convinced that he would never again run away from anything.

He fired the rifle. But he had jerked the shot, and bone fragments splintered off Touh's hard head like shrapnel as the great beast came flying.

He fired twice again. The head and horns were jumping and spitting bone chips, and Touh's silver-glistening muzzle was coming straight at Brigaud. Again Brigaud fired—straight into Touh's snout. Brigaud leaped clear as Touh's snout sprayed blood. Then the bull was down—legs kicking, body trying to roll sideways, head yanking.

Brigaud stepped in and blasted Touh's spine. It was over. Touh was dead. Brigaud felt sick. He sat down in the grass, his body shaking violently.

Brigaud sent one of the soldiers to a nearby village to fetch bearers and told the other one to sever the Cape buffalo's head. It was a barbaric act, but necessary. The Djinge and Massa tribesmen would want to see visual proof of Touh's death.

The first soldier returned with four bearers, who slung the tremendous head on long poles and started carrying it back to Fort Archambault. Bushmen from many villages came flocking after the procession as the exciting news traveled rapidly over the countryside. Everybody was laughing and capering. But Brigaud said nothing. He walked ahead of the party with his hands in his pockets.

5 THE DANGEROUS CLUB

The Caterpillar Club was originated by a parachute manufacturer on the scorched heels of one of the strangest aircraft disasters ever to happen in America. Today, nearly fifty years after the catastrophe, many hundreds of men have qualified for the club, but in 1919 the one requirement for membership was practically unheard of.

No one was ever invited to join the club, and no one who was in his right mind ever wanted to become a member. The single requirement was that a person had saved his life by the use of a parachute.

Parachutes at that time were an innovation in the flying world. They had been used sparingly in World War I—not by pilots, but by balloon observers—but no one in America had ever saved his life in an aircraft disaster by the use of one.

The manufacturer called it the Caterpillar Club because the silk that was woven into parachutes came from the cocoons that caterpillars spin. Thus, the name was a symbol; but it almost proved to be a symbolic headstone for Captain John Boettner.

A lighter-than-air blimp had been assembled in Chicago by the proprietors of an amusement park, the idea behind it being that many courageous or thrill-seeking customers would be willing to pay money to take a ride on a hydrogen airship. The blimp's name was the *Wingfoot Express* and she was completed and turned over to John Boettner on July 21, 1919.

Captain Boettner had served as pilot and instructor on lighter-than-air craft in World War I, training hundreds of army and navy observers and pilots in the use of free balloons, captive balloons, and maneuverable blimps. He had spent innumerable hours in the air, had participated in many free balloon races, and was America's most advanced advocate of lighter-than-air travel.

To Boettner, who was going to be her pilot, the *Wingfoot Express* was more beautiful than anything on man's long list of marvelous achievements. Sleek and glittery, she waited in the hot July sun for her first ascent. She had two 75-horsepower motors suspended below the swollen bag and set just behind the large open gondola. The gasbag itself was 158 feet long and was inflated by 190,000 cubic feet of hydrogen gas.

Boettner was to make the first test flight with a two-man crew: Henry Wacker, a veteran airplane mechanic, and Carl Weaver, a young mechanic who was eager to become a blimp pilot. Boettner and the two mechanics gave the *Wingfoot* a thorough going over, and then warmed up the two engines.

"Perfect," Weaver said, listening to the steady, synchronized hum of the big motors. And Wacker agreed. "Yes, they're absolutely perfect." It was a word which all three of them used again and again in their enthusiastic excitement—and all three had never been so wrong in their lives.

Everything was ready, everyone in his place. Boettner tried the controls and said famous last words to Wacker: "It's perfect. She's the perfect queen of the air." Then he turned to call overboard.

"Up ship!"

The ground crew cast off, and Boettner let the motors roar full out. The two large wooden props started pulling the big airship forward and upward and the Wing foot surged into the air, dropping the ground below like a great thrown rug. The land fell away and expanded, running off to the curvature of the earth, and the amusement park became as small as a pinwheel.

Boettner guided the *Wingfoot* low over Chicago, following along crowded streets and over sardine-packed rooftops, looking down at the thousands of little dabs of faces that were all gawking up at the "perfect" queen of the air. He throttled the motors down and they glided along on a feathery breeze. Then he climbed the ship and dived and circled and did everything except barrel-roll her. She responded as beautifully to the controls as a well-trained circus pony.

"There's no doubt about it," he called to the grinning Weaver. "She's the most perfect ship I've ever flown!"

"Right," Weaver replied. "And what perfect flying weather!"

It was indeed, so perfect that Boettner felt a reluctance about having to return to the park, where he knew there was a long line of eager customers waiting to make the first passenger flight. But they had been up for an hour now and it was time to land. He put the airship about and headed for home.

"She's perfect!" he called to the officials as the *Wingfoot* settled gently down to the earth.

"Fine," one of them replied. "But this time don't forget your parachutes."

"Parachutes?" Boettner looked blank.

"It's a company rule. Nobody goes in the gondola without a 'chute."

Boettner nodded, disgruntled about it. He was one of those "old school" pilots who believed in "fly 'em or pile 'em but don't abandon 'em." Besides that, everyone concerned with flight knew the darn things weren't reliable. This was before the time of the modern parachute which a man wears on his body and which he can open when he wants to by pulling the ripcord.

The 1919 parachutes were folded in bulky packs and hung on the outside of the blimp's gondola and were joined to the airman's harness by shroud lines. This meant that every man inside the gondola was connected to a parachute pack that was outside the gondola, which more or less created the same sort of confusion you would expect to see if three or four spiders were all trying to spin on the same web.

Just one wrong move or thoughtless turn and a couple of people would find their shroud lines in a hopeless snarl. And it was to this sort of thing that Boettner objected. He knew that a few exhibitionists had used them in America to jump out of airplanes and balloons, but secretly he was fully convinced that he would never take to a parachute except as a last resort.

"All right," he said. "Sling 'em on the side of the gondola, if you want. But those frills are just a waste of time on a perfect ship like this. Nothing is going to happen to the *Wingfoot Express*."

The parachutes were slung on the outside of the gondola, and Boettner called over the side:

"All ready for the first passengers!"

Two journalists, who had used their influence to be the first two passengers, stepped forward without the slightest idea that they were about to embark on a fateful voyage. They were both from the *Herald and Examiner*: M. G. Norton, photographer, and Earl Davenport, reporter.

They laughed and joked nervously with the ground crew, and Norton clutched his camera as though it were a baby. Neither of them had been in the air before.

"What're you gonna do if something goes wrong up there?" one of the ground crewmen kidded Davenport.

"Close my eyes and pray," Davenport said, grinning. "What else?"

"All aboard," Boettner said. "Here—get into this 'chute harness."

Davenport gave the harness and shroud lines a skeptical look.

"To tell you the truth, Captain," he said, "I'd be too scared to use that thing if I had to."

"I know how you feel," Boettner said smiling, "but it's the rules. Not that we'll have to use them, but there's always the remote chance of an accident. It can't happen in a perfect airship like this—but if it did, all you have to do is jump clear of the gondola, and the weight of your body will pull the 'chute from the pack and float you down to earth."

To set a good example, Boettner strapped himself into his parachute harness, in his heart feeling a little bit foolish and almost like a traitor to all the hundreds of men who had gone into the air before and since his time without once worrying about taking along a silly thing like a parachute.

The *Wingfoot* was ready for her first passenger flight. Boettner seated himself behind the windshield and took the controls. Weaver and Wacker sat in the stern of the gondola where they could listen to and watch their prized motors. The two passengers had seats amidship, both anxiously trying to appear as if they were not in the least nervous as they waited for the moment of takeoff.

"Don't drop your camera on some pedestrian's head when we get up there," Davenport chided his friend.

"Yeah," Norton responded, "and don't you get so rattled you forget which end of your pencil you write with."

Boettner grinned back at them and called over the side.

"Up ship!"

Again the ground crew released their holds, and for the second time that day the "perfect" airship lurched into her element and left the park, the city, the earth far below. The long flat spread of Lake Michigan extended beneath the *Wingfoot* until it looked like a fat blue finger jabbing through the crust of a green and brown pie.

Boettner took her up rapidly to an altitude of 2,000 feet and leveled off. He throttled down until they were gliding along at an average speed of forty miles per hour. The controls, the motors, the entire ship was behaving perfectly. He felt as pleased as a child with a brand-new toy.

The *Wingfoot* circled smoothly over the lake and drifted back toward the city, both motors droning in perfect synchronization. Davenport was scribbling down notes as fast as he could move his pencil; later on he would expand them into a feature story for his paper. And Norton was suddenly in his photographic paradise, leaning over the side of the gondola and clicking his camera at everything he saw. The two newsbirds were over their nervousness now, and completely enthralled by the flight.

As the *Wingfoot* came back over the city, Norton leaned forward and shouted in Boettner's ear.

"Hey, Boettner! How about flying over the Loop district so I can get some real pictures? I'll give the other newspapers something to shoot at."

It was difficult to talk above the noise of the wind and motors and so Boettner merely nodded. It suited him. When the proposed airship had first been mentioned in the newspapers, the press and the public had received the news with cynical amusement. They had rather doubted if an airship of the *Wingfoot's* size could be constructed in Chicago. Now Boettner would show them the living, flying proof.

He aimed the blimp toward the Loop—Chicago's famous business district. Minutes later Norton was crowing with delight as he leaned out and snapped one picture after another.

"This is going to be a perfect scoop on the other papers!" he told Davenport.

Boettner throttled down again, and the huge blimp was now floating along as gently as a free balloon. He wanted to give the photographer plenty of time to get his pictures. And right then—

He felt a mild thud, as though some nameless object had come out of nowhere and bumped into the pillowy gasbag. Then he heard young Weaver cry out in a horrified voice:

"Good Lord, look out!"

Boettner twisted around in his seat and literally gawked at what he saw. Little tonguelike flames were licking across the bottom of the gasbag only a few feet above their heads!

He couldn't believe it. There simply could not be a fire on his perfect airship! But it was there all right, and increasing with a *whamp-whamping* noise in the wind, and he was experienced enough to know the catastrophic explosive force of hydrogen gas. He spun around in his seat and shoved the throttles closed— but those perfect motors, faithful to the end, continued to turn over slowly.

"Jump!" Boettner yelled to the paralyzed mechanics and newsmen. "Jump—*jump!*"

He had momentarily forgotten about his own parachute. All he could think of was that they were going to blow up in a moment and the pilot was responsible for the lives of his crew and passengers. The flames were spurting from the skin of the bag, cracking out like whiplashes at the gondola below. When those 190,000 cubic feet of confined hydrogen exploded, the five of them would be blown to perdition.

Norton's professional instinct almost overruled his horror. Twice he raised his camera to snap a picture of the flames that were crawling upward on the body of the gasbag, and twice he started to jump. Then Hank Wacker caught him around the middle and hauled him to starboard and, together, they disappeared over the side of the gondola.

Frantically Boettner looked around and saw Weaver and Davenport crouching together and yelling at each other, and then Davenport jumped and Boettner lost sight of him as a finger of flame lashed at his arm. He gave his shroud lines a quick snap to straighten them, cast a glance at Weaver, and saw the youngster pile overboard in a wild leap, and then he hand-sprang out of the gondola himself.

He fell and went on falling, faster and faster, and saw the earth rushing up to meet him, and then the parachute, which he had entirely forgotten, was yanked out of the 'chute-pack and he looked up.

He was looking right into Earl Davenport's face. The reporter's shroud lines were snarled on the side of the gondola and he was dangling there and struggling helplessly. Then the flames and smoke wiped him out of Boettner's descending vision.

Abruptly Boettner's chute caught the wind and cracked open and his head was snapped back as he was jolted into an upright position. The harness held fast, the silk didn't rip, and he glided gently down toward the earth, while above him the *Wingfoot Express* twisted in flame and smoke like a flaring torch.

Far below he could see the other three parachutes floating down toward the city. Then there was a roar as the blimp exploded, and large globs of burning fabric rained around him and the motors hurtled by like sizzling comets, and the entire flaming gondola and blimp roared down, spouting smoke and fire like a geyser.

Boettner looked up and gasped. The top of his chute had caught a spark and a black hole was growing and growing in the smoldering silk as if by magic.

How long, he wondered. Good Lord, how long will it take?

But the spark died and he was suddenly so glad to be alive that he wanted to cry and shout, and he started to do both when he looked down again. . . .

There was a quick flash of flame below him and Norton's parachute vanished in a wink of the eye. That was all; one moment it was a parachute, and the next it was a puff of smoke and the tiny figure of the photographer was plummeting head-over-heels into the yawning city.

Young Weaver's parachute caught a spark and the gasoline on it ignited. When he had almost reached the first of the tall roofs, his parachute flared like a match. Almost instantly he was swung against the side of the Western Union Building and knocked senseless. His parachute disappeared in a flash and he dropped to his death in the street.

Hank Wacker collided with the cornice of a rearing building and was knocked out. He piled down onto a fire escape and sprawled there, unconscious but without a single broken bone.

Boettner was the last down and he had his own problems. Just as he saw the flaming mass of the airship crash into the Loop, the sharp spire of a skyscraper loomed under his feet. At first he thought he could land on it, but he changed his mind when he saw that there was no footing for him on its steeply pitched sides.

Hastily he seesawed as his shroud lines spun half about and barely missed the skyscraper, glided on by, and watched the flat roof of the next building coming up at him. His feet hit with a jolt that drove all the breath out of his lungs, and he went over in a somersault and realized he was being dragged helplessly into a large glass skylight.

At that moment his gasoline-and-oil-soaked parachute burst into flames that billowed toward him in a rooftop breeze, and he crawled in panic around the edge of the skylight, his fingers fumbling with the buckles on the parachute harness. He was out of it— free—standing on his feet and alive.

Badly shaken and only dazedly conscious of the fact that he had barely escaped a ghastly death, he was helped down to the street by some incredulous office workers. It was only then that he became fully aware of the tragic outcome of the blimp's doomed flight.

The entire wreckage of the *Wingfoot Express*—motors, gas tanks, gondola, the flaming envelope of the gasbag—all of it had crashed through the flat roof of a large bank, spewing and exploding fiery oil and gasoline far and wide, creating a screaming inferno inside the bank that took ten lives and seriously injured a score of others.

The "perfect" airship's toll was thirteen dead. Boettner got off with a burned arm, and Wacker had a bump on his head. This grim disaster was what gave the parachute manufacturer the idea for the Caterpillar Club. Wacker and Boettner were both presented with the first two pins, each with his name and number engraved on the back of the pin. Wacker, who had beat Boettner down by two seconds, became Caterpillar Number One; Boettner was Caterpillar Number Two.

Hank Wacker gave up all ideas of flight after the *Wingfoot* disaster, but Captain Boettner went on to put in over 10,000 hours in lighter-than-air ships without a single accident. He continued to be the advance advocate of the airship—and, of course, of the parachutes that were made with the caterpillars' help.

6 A FEW GRAINS OF SAND

A sudden current pushed a fuzzy-booking grappling line along the side of the sunken submarine. As it undulated, snakelike, past the two Navy salvage divers, it brushed Tom Eadie's helmet window. He reacted with a start, and nearly lost his balance.

"It's only a line," he told himself. But he was unnerved and he knew it. Too many things had been happening to divers on this salvage job, and some of the men were starting to grumble about a "hoodoo sub."

The sub in question was the S-51, which had sunk in twenty-two fathoms of water in 1926, fourteen miles east of Block Island. The U.S. Navy had placed Commander Edward Ellsberg in charge of salvage operations, instructing him to seal up the sub, pump her dry, and refloat her. Ten divers had started out on the job, but five of them were now useless from sheer exhaustion, plus a few cases of the "bends," and one was dying in the hospital from oxygen stimulation. There also had been a misfortune that occurred only a few days ago.

Petty Officer L'Heureux, a new diver, was going down to the S-51 with veteran diver Joe Eiben. L'Heureux's job was to hold a 1,000-watt submarine lamp so that Joe could see to work in the S-51's engine room. Dressed in their Gargantuan rigs —the bulky twill and rubber-lined suits, the massive lead shoes and weight belts, and the huge Cyclopean copper helmets—Joe and L'Heureux went over the side and down the descending line.

A few minutes later, Tom Eadie was encased in his suit, had his helmet screwed on, and went overboard to follow them down. He passed slowly through the upper sun-illuminated waters, into the opaque twilight world, and then descended into the dark gloom of the sea floor.

At a hundred and thirty feet he reached the deck of the S-51, touching down just before the conning tower. L'Heureux was standing by the deck gun in a fixed position, holding up his blazing light like the Statue of Liberty.

Wondering if anything was wrong with him, Eadie clapped L'Heureux on the back and placed his own helmet against the other diver's helmet. Deep-sea divers can communicate in this manner, because their voices will resound through the copper.

"Are you all right?" Eadie asked. "Yes," was L'Heureux's reply. Reassured, Eadie plodded on to his own job. What he didn't know was that L'Heureux was suffering from oxygen-intoxication. He didn't know what he was doing or saying, and he had completely lost sense of direction.

Meanwhile, Joe Eiben was still waiting inside the inky-black engine room wondering when L'Heureux was coming with the light. Finally, he phoned the telephone tender up on the salvage boat, wanting to know if L'Heureux was coming or not? Puzzled, Commander Ellsberg took the headset and transmitted on L'Heureux's phone and tried to contact him. No answer. Ellsberg then switched over to Eadie's phone and ordered him to go aft and find L'Heureux.

Eadie left his work in the bows of the S-51 and proceeded aft along the forward deck. He didn't see L'Heureux, but he bumped into Joe Eiben who had been coming from the aft. They put their helmets together to discuss the mystery.

Each had proceeded from either end of the sub and now they had met amidships, but L'Heureux wasn't between them. What had happened to him? Where had he gone?

Anxiously, Eadie looked around in the gloomy depths. Then he gave a start. A small glow of light was flickering in the liquid dark about a hundred feet off the S-51's starboard beam. It was moving farther away on the bottom all the time!

Eadie started down the side of the sub, with Joe playing out his lifeline to give him support. On the bottom, Eadie leaned into the water and started plodding after the light. The floor was sand and it was flat and bare, and Eadie felt like a man wandering into a vast empty desert at midnight.

When Eadie finally caught up with him, L'Heureux

was blundering around in a great confused circle, going nowhere, and holding up his lamp like Diogenes seeking for a glimmer of truth in a dark world. A halo of small popeyed fish were circling around his head, as if wondering what in the world he was doing there.

The oxygen intoxication was bad enough, but what happened to L'Heureux when they brought him up to the salvage boat was far worse. He doubled over suddenly with a severe case of the bends. The decompression tank seemed to have no effect on the crippled diver. He was paralyzed, unconscious, and the navy surgeon feared for his life. The salvage boat headed for Newport and L'Heureux was rushed to the Naval Hospital where the doctors barely managed to pull him through.

Now there were only Eadie and Joe Eiben and two other divers left to manage the Herculean task of sealing the S-51—and Eadie was beginning to wonder exactly what might happen next.

What they were trying to do now was to dig a tunnel through the mud and sand under the sub; a difficult and very spooky chore. They had to lie flat on the sand in a tight watery tunnel beneath the S-51, in total darkness, and blast their way through the sand and mud and icy water with a pressured stream of water blown from a fire-hose nozzle.

For an hour now Eadie had been squirming in that narrow black trap with the steel skin of the sub pressing on his back, working more by feeling than by sight. Then he felt Joe shake his left foot and he cut off the power of the fire hose and backed out of the hole.

Joe's form came up to him and he rubbed his copper helmet against his partner's. Eadie could hear the tinny ring of Joe's voice.

"Our hour is up. Let's go topside. I'm feeling kind of jumpy down here."

It suited Eadie. He was feeling the same way. To get up into the clear crisp air, to sprawl out on the sunny deck with a cigarette and a cup of java sounded better right then than a month's pay. Together, they stepped onto the small steel decompressing stage that would lift them to the surface.

The stage was a grilled affair, the platform about six by six. It was suspended on a cable from the end of the salvage boat's boom. Eadie pressed the chin-push in his helmet for the "speak" position on the loud-speaker telephone, and heard the buzz of the trans-mitter-receiver diaphragm in the crown of his helmet.

"On deck," he said. "Bring us up."

The stage began to lift cautiously. The two divers stood relaxed inside their clumsy suits of two-ply tanned twill, their heads peanutlike within the great copper shells. A thin current pushed at them and the stage wobbled slightly.

Looking down, Eadie watched the wrecked S-51 with its covering of marl fall away below them. Abruptly the pale outline of the submarine blurred and then disappeared.

At ninety feet below the surface and forty-five feet above the ocean floor, the stage came to a pause.

This was the first decompression level. Eadie and Joe went into a vigorous exercise routine, like two savages dancing around a ritual tom-tom. This was done to stimulate their circulations and to speed up the elimination of nitrogen from their systems.

Hanging there in the void, the two divers did deep-knee bends, working side by side. They were both veteran divers and "staging" in an ascent was purely a matter of everyday routine. They paid no attention to each other.

Suddenly Eadie realized that something was wrong, very wrong. The automatic exhaust valve in his helmet had jammed closed. Before he could gather his wits, the thing that every deep-sea diver feared happened. He was "blowing up." His suit—the air release now blocked—began to swell. Its buoyancy multiplied rapidly and Eadie started to drift upward.

He made a hurried motion to try to open the control valve on his breastplate to shut off the incoming air. Too late—his gloved hand never reached the valve. His entire suit had suddenly stiffened out from internal pressure.

His arms went straight out from his sides like a man about to make a swan dive. He was spread-eagled and shooting for the surface, ninety feet above. Frantically he shouted into his phone transmitter.

"Turn off my air on deck!"

Would his telephone tender on board the salvage boat understand the startling and unnatural order? Would he comply in time? Probably not; because what tender would want to take it upon himself to cut off a diver's air (a diver's only pipeline with life) when he was ninety feet under the sea?

For a wild second, terrifying possibilities crowded into Eadie's brain and kept him momentarily witless. His quick ascent after such a long deep dive would give him the bends. But worse—the suspended stage which he had just left was dangling from the boom beneath the salvage boat's side, and he was shooting straight up for the bottom of that boat, propelled like a cannonball by buoyancy. When he struck the hull of the boat it would flatten him out, helmet and all.

"On deck!" he cried. "I'm blo—"

He was zooming upward, totally helpless. The top of the steel bail, which supported the suspended stage, flashed down before his grid-window. It was impossible to bring his air-stretched arms inward to clutch it, but he knew he could still kick his legs out from the waist.

He shoved his weighted feet toward the triangle at the apex of the bail. The brass toe caps on his shoes caught. His body came to a halt and he cried out as pain shot up from his strained ankles. He hung that way, by his toe caps, with the rapidly increasing buoyancy of his bulging suit straining and tugging to tear him loose and shoot him upward again.

He leaned his head forward and banged his chin against the exhaust valve in his helmet. Hopeless. Grimacing his face into an ugly mask, he tried to force his arms to bend in to the control valve. Impossible. He opened his mouth to yell into the teletransmitter again—and then everything went crazy.

The consistently hammering air coming from the relentless compressors pressurized the already distended suit almost to its limit. The shoulder harness that held his helmet and breastplate to his waistbelt snapped under the expanding strain. The twill suit stretched upward and the helmet and breastplate leaped past his head, the copper lid of the breastplate slamming on his jaw, leaving him stunned and bleeding. He gasped, his brain skyrocketing, and spat a thick spray of warm blood.

He was out of his helmet now—his entire body was inside the twill-and-rubber suit! The copper helmet was a dark, rounded orb, fully two feet above his head. The eighty-pound waistbelt, no longer supported, dropped down to his ankles. The incoming air swelled the suit further, stretching his toe-hooked body until he felt like an Inquisition victim on a torture rack.

He was caught in a tight grip of pain. The air pressure was still rapidly climbing, increasing the flow of blood that was already dribbling from his mouth and nose. He tilted back his head and looked up into the shadowy helmet. The teletransmitter was his only hope and he yelled at it.

"On deck! I've blown up! Tell Joe to climb up to me, shut off my air, and open my petcock!" But he knew it was futile. The helmet and transmitter were too far away. The tender on deck would never hear him.

The pressure inside the suit multiplied pound after pound and his eardrums began to ring and throb and the blood sprayed from his mouth and nose and the strain on his feet was unbearable. It was the end, he knew. His toe caps would tear loose in a moment and he would rocket for the surface—and death.

Suddenly his suit exploded!

The fabric of his small copper and twill suit ripped before his face, directly under the breastplate, and for a split second a great glassy bubble bulged in the tear and he saw the wall of the sea, distorted and unreal.

Then it was gone and the deflated suit shriveled in on him and with it came the clutching pressure of the sea. Icy water smashed into his bleeding face and filled his torn suit, the heavy helmet dropped back over his head, and his body twisted in pain from the sudden reversal of tension. He felt as if he were in a giant vise, and his eardrums, sinuses, and lungs formed a vacuum. His buoyancy now gone, the lead and copper weight of his diving rig plunged him downward.

His toe caps lost their grip on the steel bail and Eadie went straight down like a stove and struck the grill of the diving stage with a great clump, nearly knocking over his startled partner.

Half senseless, trapped in a torn and flooded suit, he lay in a half-drowned tangle of ripped twill, flapping harness, twisted lead and copper, doing his best to keep from swallowing saltwater.

He could see Joe's shocked face behind the grid-window, as his partner stooped over him, and saw his mouth moving, sending instructions to the deck, and felt Joe's hands under his armpits, trying to bring him into an upright position, and he heard the heavy wheeze of the intake in his helmet. Would the incoming air have enough force to hold the rising water away from his face?

It has to, he thought dazedly. More! More air!

Abruptly the helmet yanked and he felt that he was rising. He left the diving stage and Joe below. They were hauling him up by his lines. But he knew he was still in a very bad way.

The suit was torn halfway across the chest; water-logged, filled to the brim, it and the heavy shoes and the lead belt were working against him, causing a downward drag. The helmet and breastplate were drawing him upward, both straining against the un-harnessed suit. If the ruptured twill let go completely, the shoes and belt and waterlogged suit would ballast him helplessly to the bottom. His head would come out of the helmet like a pea from a pod and he would be crushed to a jelly by the pressure.

At least he had hooked his feet to the steel bail in an attempt to save himself, and that had been worth something. He hadn't simply given in and let himself be blown up to the surface like a cork from a champagne bottle. His head sagged against the side of the helmet and he began to retch in the water that was trying to seep past his chin.

Vaguely, he saw blurred sunlight and the two relief divers standing on the auxiliary stage. They were reaching for him. He felt hands, heard a vast endless ringing, tasted salt and blood. He was being lifted. Water was splashing somewhere. He felt more hands.

Unconsciousness surged toward him. Hands were doing things to him, voices were shouting. The wall retreated and he was semiconscious again. He was flat on his back on the deck of the salvage boat. Up through the grid-window of his helmet he could see the clear turquoise oval of sky. Voices and hands . . . hands and voices. . . .

"Don't bother getting the helmet and breastplate off. Cut his shoes loose and pull him right out through the hole in the suit!"

"Get him in the decompression tank. I've never seen a diver blow up this bad before!"

"What was the matter with you, Joe? Couldn't you see him blowing up and grab his feet to stop him as he went by you?"

"Yes, Commander. I saw him go by me out of the corner of my faceplate, but I just figured he was making an extra high jump and I went right on exercising."

Then they had Eadie in the decompression tank and ran up fifty pounds of air pressure on him while the surgeon went to work on him. A couple of hours later they had him wrapped in blankets in his bunk below. Commander Ellsberg came in to see him with a smile.

"You're a lucky man, Tom. The doc says you'll live to dive again."

"I can't understand what happened to my exhaust valve," Eadie said. "It was working fine right till we started to come up."

"I've disassembled your valve and found the trouble," Ellsberg said. "Evidently while you were lying in the mud in the tunnel, some muddy water washed into your helmet on one side of your valve while the exhaust air was blowing out the other side. It left a little sand in the valve housing, and when you started to come up, the sand lodged in the valve sleeve and jammed the valve stem."

The commander paused and shook his head.

"That's all it took, Tom. Just a few little grains of sand you can hardly see without a microscope, but they came within a hairsbreadth of killing you."

7 FORT NUMBER FOUR

The Moroccan dawn was sticky, hot, oppressive, as if the end of the departing night were lashing up the heat from the dark desert sands. There had been no moon, the stars were dimmed by haze, and inside Fort Number Four it was as dark as a pit. For in that far outpost beyond civilization there were adequate reasons just then why a display of lights would not have been healthy.

Privates J. McQueen-Desmond and Richard Jordan went up the ladder to the firing step for the morning stand-to. They were both young British ex-servicemen who had fought in France in World War I. Hearing that Spain intended to penetrate and pacify the savage Moroccan interior, and feeling an urge for adventure in an exotic land, they had enlisted in the Spanish Foreign Legion in 1920.

Their idea of exotic adventure soon lost its enchantment when they were sent to a small mud fort on the southern fringe of Spanish-occupied territory. The outpost stood at the apex of four caravan routes which converged into a single road running north to the sea. Their job was to guard this lonely road from the marauding Riffs—the barbaric and warlike Arab tribesmen.

The fort was a three-roomed blockhouse surrounded by a sturdy mud wall in a tirangular shape. A broad firing platform ran around the inner side of the wall for the Legion riflemen, and a Lewis machine gun was situated at each of the three corners. There were one hundred and fifty Legionnaires in the little garrison and twenty-three of them were Britons—volunteers like Desmond and Jordan.

The livestock inside the fort compound had long since been eaten and the troops were subsisting on flesh of a kind not deemed tasty by epicures—rats. All supplies were low and scurvy was prevalent. And worse—for weeks a certain turbulent and bloodthirsty tribe of Riffs had been knocking at the front door with bullets.

Desmond and Jordan leaned against their firing loopholes and conversed in low tones as the purple African sun went shooting up in the east.

"Well," Jordan muttered wearily, "whose turn is it to go fetch the water today?"

"Theirs, I am relieved to say."

The Spanish lack of military efficiency was appalling to the two young men and their twenty-one English comrades. Not only had the Spaniards miscalculated on their livestock and supplies, but they had made absolutely no provision for water inside the fort! Every day an armed fatigue party had to haul barrels in a wagon to a well that was *a mile away from the fort* in order to fetch the vital water. And of course they were sniped at coming and going by the Arabs lurking among the dunes.

The Spaniards, for some reason, looked down upon the British volunteers and had as little to do with them as possible. They isolated them in one platoon under a sergeant named Lockesley, and when it was the British platoon's turn to escort the water wagon, the Spanish commander sent the twenty-three of them out into the treacherous sands.

Yet when it was the Spaniards' turn to fetch the water, the commander and his one hundred and twenty-six Legionnaires all went, leaving the twenty-three Englishmen to hold the fort!

"I don't know how much longer we can hold out." Desmond said to his friend. "There must be hundreds of Riffs crawling around the dunes out there by now."

As if to punctuate his statement, some nearby Arab sniper fired his rifle and the bullet ricocheted off the top of the wall into the sky. It served as a vivid reminder of the watchful nearness of the Riffs.

"With Fort Number Three only thirty miles west you'd wonder that we haven't been relieved by now," Jordan said, staring out at the stark whiteness of the desert.

Yes, Desmond had been wondering—wondering and praying. The Riffs had cut their telephone line two weeks ago, and he reasoned that the fort's long silence would cause the rest of the Spanish brigade to suspect that something had happened at Fort Number Four and send a relief column to investigate.

But nothing happened. As far as the outside world was concerned, they might as well have been marooned on an uncharted island in the middle of an ocean.

There was a nearby foothill, from which normally they could contact Fort Three by heliograph. But now it was suicide to try to send a signaling party to the top of it long enough to begin communication—the Riff snipers were behind every rock and bush.

The commander had sent a runner out under cover of darkness—and the next morning the garrison found his body. No more runners were sent.

It was in anticipation of a dread doom that Desmond had been praying that the besieged little garrison would soon be relieved. He was a professional soldier and he gave no outward sign of his anxiety, but already in his active imagination he was facing the horror of his own death.

Morning was here and the Spanish commander lined up his one hundred and twenty-six men to escort the water wagon to the distant well.

"Sergeant," the commanding officer called to Lockesley, "take charge of the post. We will be back before noon."

"But, sir," Lockesley said, "Lieutenant Vargas has issued my platoon only ten rounds of ammunition per man, and none for the machine guns."

"That's quite sufficient," the Spanish officer said impatiently. "Just carry out your orders, Sergeant. Don't question them." And, turning abruptly away, he called, "March the company out, Lieutenant!"

As the gate swung open, a sniper's bullet hit the blockhouse wall. The Spanish company marched out of the fort, dragging along the barrel wagon, and the gate shut behind them. Lockesley stood in the sun-parched compound and cursed quietly.

"That idiot has all the rest of the ammunition locked in a compartment in the blockhouse," he complained to a soldier named Evans. "And here we are without enough ammo among us to even fight off a squad of Boy Scouts, let alone five or six hundred Riffs!"

The twenty-three English soldiers lined the tri-angular walls—seven men to a side with Lockesley and a corporal making the rounds—and stared anxiously at the great sea of bare sand that surrounded them.

A sniper bullet hit the compound, and then more and more of them began to pock the mud walls. Desmond crouched at his loophole, searching the dunes sprawling before him.

The noise of sniper bullets began to increase in tempo. and suddenly a soldier next to the wall dropped with a clatter, stumbled back from his loophole, and plunged headlong into the sand below the wall. Another soldier simply slumped face-down in his loop-hole without a sound, as if he had suddenly dropped to sleep at his post.

"Keep down!" Lockesley ordered. "Don't fire back unless you see a Riff and you're certain you can hit him. We've precious little ammo as it is."

During the past two weeks the observant Arabs had been studying the garrison's pattern of duty: one morning twenty-three Legionnaires went for water, one hundred and twenty-seven marched out and the twenty-three stayed in the fort. The obvious strategy, therefore, was to attack the fort when it was defended by only the twenty-three Britons. For days now the Riffs had been collecting a mighty horde of warriors around the outpost. . . .

The Spanish Legionnaires had passed out of sight around a shoulder of the hill, and in the next instant the desert was swarming with Riffs, swiftly and silently advancing to attack.

"The Arabs!" Desmond yelled. "Stand to! Stand to!"

Looking out again he saw the scattered fringe of warriors blend into lines and the lines into masses of swiftly running Riffs, and then their deep menacing war cry came down on the little mud fort with a growing roar.

The expanding swarm of Riffs swept out to the left, to the right, to surround the fort on three sides. Watching them coming on, Desmond estimated that there must have been five hundred of them already in sight.

"Open fire!" Lockesley bawled. "Rapid fire! Here —you and you—break open the door to the ammo dump!"

Desmond opened fire, his sights on the running, robed figures, firing a round, seeing a white-clad man fall like a sack and lie motionless on the sand, firing again and again.

The Arabs pressed forward in an orderly advance, not in a blind charge: coming on in short rushes from rock to dune, a hundred at a time, while the rest of them sprawled along the dunes on all sides of the fort and poured in a steady fire which raked the mud walls.

The British were falling around Desmond as he bolted and sighted and fired, and the withering Riff fire was hitting on both sides of his loophole, embrasure, and, as he watched the running, sprawling, shooting Riffs surge forward, brandishing their long, straight swords and waving their war lances, he knew that he and his handful of comrades couldn't hope to hold them back.

With Riffs pumping bullets into the fort's embrasures, a hundred others attacked the gate with stones, axes, and swords. The rest swarmed right up to the foot of the walls and made human ladders of themselves. Climbing, scrambling—all wild eyes and white teeth and glinting sword blades—they came yelling up the walls.

The two soldiers in the compound couldn't break down the door to the ammo dump in time. Without the three Lewis guns to spray the embattled walls, the British didn't stand a chance. The Riffs were scrabbling up over the parapets and through the embrasures. There were only a dozen defenders still on their feet to meet them with the bayonets.

There was no question of surrender or quarter in anyone's mind.

Just then a great bawling Riff topped the wall in a wild leap and rushed at Desmond with his huge sword cocked over his shoulder. In that split second Desmond was aware that the Arabs had spilled over all three walls and through the shattered gate. He knew he was the last defender standing, and he remembered that he had one round left in his rifle.

Baring his teeth, he thrust his bayonet squarely against the lunging Riff's chest and jerked the trigger. It was the last shot fired in the fort.

The huge Riff's impetus toppled him forward. As Desmond instinctively sprang back to get out of his way, he stepped into space. He had missed the edge of the platform!

He plunged ten feet into the compound and cracked his head.

Coming back to life was like swimming up from the bottom of a deep pool of pain. Then he opened his eyes and realized he had been thrown into the storeroom inside the blockhouse.

It was a shock to find that he was still alive; and when he sat up he was startled to see that Richard Jordan, Sergeant Locklesley, the cockney Evans, and two others were in the room with him. Jordan crawled over to him. He, like all of them, had been slashed and bruised but not badly wounded.

"I didn't think you were ever coming around," he said. "We're all that's left. The other seventeen are dead."

"How come they haven't killed us?"

Jordan made a wry face. "Saving us for torture. Lockesley knows a little Arabic and he's been listening to our guards. Seems they intend to mutilate us when they find the time for it. You know how they are."

Numbly, Desmond nodded. He knew how the Riffs were. A shiver ran up his spine, and he wished that he had been killed in the battle. In a little while, Lockesley came away from the open doorway.

"From what I get out of their yammering," he said, "the bunch that jumped us were an advance guard of a big Riff army that is moving northward to drive the Spaniards into the sea. There are only about fifty of them in the fort now. The rest have gone out to mop up our Simple Simon CO and his troops."

Occasionally an Arab guard would look in at the prisoners and spit at them. The heat in the blockhouse was terrible. When they asked for water, the Riffs laughed at them. Desmond's cut head put him in agony.

The parched, painful night dragged toward dawn. Desmond had almost come to the end of his senses when the Arabs started yelling in the compound. A couple of rifles cracked, and then a machine gun started to fire against the wall.

"That's one of the Lewis guns," Jordan said. "Somebody must be attacking the fort!"

Two Riffs were jabbering excitedly near the doorway, and Lockesley was listening. A minute later he joined his five comrades and told them the news.

"Well, mates, I guess we'll know all the answers soon. They were saying something about 'inglés.' That must mean that the Brigade has sent a column of British volunteers to relieve us. The Riffs hope to hang on here until their main force turns up, but our boys will swamp this mud.pie in a hurry. And that means we can wish ourselves good night."

Desmond knew what he meant. If the Arabs saw that they were going to lose the fort, they would first put their six prisoners to the sword. And what could they, the unarmed prisoners, do about it?

The sporadic fire around the fort soon turned into a continuous roll of crashing sound. All three Lewis guns were firing now, and volley after volley of musketry exploded in the dawn. Without warning, a gang of Riffs rushed into the room and piled onto the struggling prisoners. The six battered British soldiers tried to put up a fight, but the Arabs simply swarmed over them. They were yanked and kicked out into the compound and bound together in pairs, back to back. Desmond found himself tied to the cockney Evans.

Abusing the helpless men, the Arabs dragged them up the ladders to the firing platform and shoved them against the bullet-ridden parapet, placing them directly in the line of fire from the advancing Legionnaires.

The bullets snapped along the parapet. One of them grazed Desmond's upper arm and landed in Evan's back. The cockney gasped and went limp.

"Des!"

Desmond realized that Jordan was calling him, and when he looked around he saw that his best friend was already sagging in his bonds, leaning against an embrasure with blood dripping from his clenched mouth.

"We'll show 'em how Englishmen die, eh boy?" Jordan cried. Then he too went limp.

The outraged Arabs shoved Desmond and the dead weight that was strapped to him higher, and the bullets sang around the living man and his dead comrade. At least two more bullets struck Evan's body before one of them finally hit Desmond's thigh. The pain made him sick and he lost his equilibrium.

The next thing he knew the Arabs had pulled him

down and rolled Evans and himself into the compound below. Fortunately, he landed on top of Evans, but even so the shattering jar of the fall nearly spun him over the brink of unconsciousness.

Dazed, he realized that two Arabs were trying to haul him into the blockhouse. Not able to budge him with the dead weight of Evans on his back, they cut him loose from the bleeding corpse, grabbed him by the ankles, dragged him bumpily across the sand, and flung him into the storehouse.

A moment later Lockesley and a private named Hart were heaved bodily into the room. Both appeared to be wounded; Hart was barely breathing.

Desmond's eyes were closed and his mind seemed to whirl crazily. Then he realized that Lockesley was tugging at him.

"Hey, Desmond, wake up, man. Wake up. Get over here, back of these date sacks."

Desmond didn't seem to have the strength left in his battered body to move. When he struggled into a sitting position, the pain in his leg grabbed like a white-hot pincer. Painfully, he dragged himself across the sandy floor and got behind the pile of date sacks with Lockesley.

"The perishing Riffs are catching it good now," Lockesley said in a tense voice. "They'll lose this mousetrap any time, and they'll not forget to put *paid* to us when they do. If we only had a weapon!"

Desmond nodded and looked around. There were many boxes of stores stacked around them, but he knew most of them were empty. He noticed a wooden box under some hardtack crates and, dizzily, he tried to focus his dimming eyes on the faded words that had been stenciled on the end of the box. . . .

Mills Bombs.

He crawled over to the empty hardtack boxes and shoved them aside. The Mills box had already been opened and he saw it was half full of hand grenades.

"Look here, Sarge. Grenades!"

Lockesley couldn't make it. "Fetch 'em over."

Desmond tossed three or four of the small bombs into the sand by Lockesley. Taking one in each hand, he wriggled back to the date sacks and lined all of them up on the little gunnysack barricade before them.

The volume of machine-gun and rifle fire increased until it became almost deafening. The battle raging outside was reaching a violent climax.

"Get ready to feed 'em to the devils when they come for us," Lockesley said.

Desmond raised his tortured body into a half-upright position so that he could peg his grenades at the door. He pulled the cotter pin on the first one and compressed the activating spring lever with his sweating hand. Let them come soon, he prayed.

The Lewis gun mounted in the northeast corner suddenly stopped. There was a great yelling, and four or five howling Riffs piled up in the doorway with raised swords.

"Now!" Lockesley cried, and the two British soldiers lobbed their grenades at the oncoming Riffs.

In the gray smoke and the yellow flash of flame, Desmond pegged grenade after grenade as fast as he could pull the pin and toss. In the rapid series of explosions crashing one upon another, he felt as though volcanoes were erupting under his body. Then, almost without warning, the world suddenly turned over on him.

It was noon when he regained consciousness. He was lying on an army cot in a hospital and Lockesley was on another cot beside him.

"Our boys carried the fort while we were pitching bombs," Lockesley told him. He grinned weakly. "I guess we did too good a job. We nearly wrecked the blockhouse. The roof and a couple of walls fell on top of us."

"What about Hart?" Desmond wondered.

"He was dead when they pulled us out of the rubble. You and me are all that's left."

Desmond and Lockesley were the only two survivors of the twenty-three valiant British soldiers who had fought to hold on to Fort Number Four. Did they receive thanks for their valor? They did not. The Spanish Foreign Legion had peculiar views when it came to expressing appreciation for heroics.

The commander of the fort had managed to get his one hundred and twenty-six men away from the attacking Riffs (thereby leaving the twenty-three besieged British soldiers to their fate), and had reached the Brigade headquarters. He then turned in a report that was instrumental in getting for Desmond and Lockesley a severe reprimand from higher up—for having lost the fort to the Riffs!

8 SHARK SILENCE

The old Ford with the numerous dents in its fenders and doors rattled through a brilliant green mangrove stand and turned into a sequestered little bay near Grassy. George Robbins, a young Australian fishtrap man, halted his truck near a creek and got out on the damp ground, smiling.

There had been a storm the night before, and that was just what he needed to drive the fish from the neighboring creeks into his trap in the bay. He had a cage-trap at the mouth of a deep tidal creek on the coast of Australia, and this day was his market day.

He paused for a moment, staring out at his place of business with a satisfied eye. Below the tangled mangroves and the bright ribbon of beach the bay was like a giant feathered disk, fluttering in the morning breeze. Far out across the water was the low purple line of the Great Barrier Reef.

The bay was the type of workshop Robbins liked —isolated and void of people. No one ever came there except himself and the fish. He didn't like to be gawked at by noisy tourists, or to have fishermen cadging fish off him for bait.

He kept a rowboat—which he called his "flatty" —on the beach, and he rowed out to his trap. It was made of sturdy wire mesh and all of it was exposed at low tide. Two long wire fences spread winglike from either bank of the creek and stretched two-hundred feet into the bay where they joined at the trap. This helped to channel the creek fish into the cages.

There were two cages, one behind the other, connected by a narrow wire funnel. Each cage was six feet high and six feet wide and had a wire gate in a wooden frame at the back. They and the fences were set on a flat coral reef and all the securing stakes had been driven by Robbins' hand into the rock-hard coral.

It was an ideal prison for fish, as the cages were completely covered with water at high tide, and even at low tide there was enough water on the reef to keep most of his catch alive for days.

The flatty moved out into the placid little bay and scuttled around the left-hand fence. Robbins wanted to empty out the main cage first. Approaching it now at low tide, his face brightened with pleasure when he saw all the barramunda, groper, trevally, salmon, and butterfish he had netted. This promised to be the best market day in his fishing career.

He paused at the back of the main cage, looking cautiously around for sharks, and then climbed overboard and unhooked the wire fasteners on the gate and waded waist-deep into his cage. The silver trevally and the fat butterfish swished and wriggled around and through his legs in panic. He went to work with his scoop.

The scoop was wire mesh, three feet long by two

wide. It was a Herculean task to handle the thing with big fish in it, but at least it was large enough to hold them and it let the water out. He was dumping thrashing fish of all sizes and kinds into his flatty when he suddenly spotted a dangerous intruder.

Close at hand a deadly black-spotted conger eel shot out of a fissure in the coral floor. Its needle-rimmed jaws were agape and its eyes flashed at all the darting fish.

Robbins slammed his empty scoop at the water, but it had no effect on the five-foot killer. Retreating to his flatty, he got an oar. Reaching the eight-foot ash sweep through the gate, he jabbed at the conger, hoping to frighten it away.

If the conger decided to remain in one of the coral cracks on the floor of the cage, Robbins was in trouble. He couldn't work with it nearby because if the conger should grab his ankle with its powerful toothy jaws, not even ten strong men would be able to pull the eel from its hole. Robbins would be trapped inside his own cage; and when the high tide came he would drown.

But he was in luck. The conger didn't like the probing oarblade. It took one quick vicious snap at the wood and then snaked away in a swift streak.

Robbins waded into his cage again. The incident had cost him precious time and he would have to work hard to make up for it. He still had to empty both traps, row his catch ashore, transfer it to the lorry by wheelbarrow, and then drive his fish to the nearest town.

He went to work with a will, scooping the fish into

his boat until he had the main cage empty. Now for the receiving cage in front.

The water around the receiving cage was so shallow he didn't have enough clearance to float his flatty with its heavy cargo of fish. It meant he was going to be stuck with a lot of extra wading and lugging. Nothing else to do for it, though. He threw out an anchor and splashed over to the gate with his scoop.

The surface of the receiving cage was blistered with the bodies of floating dead fish, all smelling. This frequently happened when there was an exceptionally low tide and the sun was extremely hot. Some of the large fish couldn't sustain life in the shallow warm water.

He started pitching the dead fish out through the gate, never dreaming how desperately he was shortly going to need those smelly carcasses. The incoming tide washed them away.

Just as he was ready to commence scooping he spotted another bit of bad luck. There was a large hole in the narrow funnelway and another one in the cage itself. Evidently a monster turtle or a big groper had blundered into the trap and one or the other had caused the damage to the wire with its teeth.

"More time lost," he muttered in annoyance.

He waded to his boat and got a small bale of mending wire and a pair of wire cutters and returned to the cage. More trouble! The hole in the funnel was underwater and an eagle ray was in there looking for a way out—and Robbins had a hard time helping him to find it!

The ray had a sting in its tail a foot long and it flashed this way, that way, then zagged in the water to lash at the man's legs. It kept him hopping about dodging the vicious sting, until with a sudden lucky lunge he managed to get the slippery creature by the eye sockets.

Lashing and flapping wildly in the air from the end of the man's outstretched arm, the ray was finally pitched through the gateway. Gasping for breath, Robbins went to work on the hole.

It took him longer to mend the rent than he had expected, and then there was still the one in the receiving cage to attend to. Time lost or not, it had to be done before the next tide when the fish would come across the reef in search of food, or he would lose all of his next catch.

Now, as he hurriedly waded into the receiving cage, the tide was already rising with a rapidity that worried him. Seemed as though his promising day was determined to go sour.

The torn wire was badly twisted and he had to splice the mending wire to one of the upright steel stakes to get it to hold—and in his haste he dropped the wire cutters outside the cage.

"One thing after another!" he growled.

Now he would have to wade all the way around both cages to get the cutters! He straightened up with the fixed look of a hard-pressed man who is harassed beyond reason. And the incoming tide certainly didn't help his temperament. The sea had been less than knee-deep when he first entered the cage; now it was nearly waist-high. He was running short of time. And short of luck, too.

The wire cage shuddered under a sudden terrific impact. He looked up, startled.

A large peaked fin was in the water.

A twelve-foot tiger shark, hanging sleek-bodied and swollen with its pectorals extended in the water, was just outside the cage. It stared at the stunned man with a round glassy eye.

Robbins started backing away from the wire wall. It was time to get out of there and get to the flatty but, he had left his boat nearly twenty feet from the cage. And that wasn't all. When he looked across the rising surface, he saw that the boat was dragging its anchor—slowly drifting shoreward!

The hungry tiger shark whipped the water with its tail and slammed head-on into the wire again. The entire cage trembled under the blow and the wire bulged inward as the trapped fish darted and collided around Robbins in a frenzy.

The water was over his waist, and he looked around with a stark expression. For a moment he couldn't believe it, didn't want to accept the fact that the sea was rising to the level of the gate. He looked up at the tough wire mesh that covered the top of the cage.

The flatty looked miles away, and he cursed himself for not having tried to bring it closer to the cage. Wildly, he looked around for his cutters. There they were on the coral shelf, only inches beyond the wire. Maybe he could get his fingers far enough through the wire to drag them back.

If he could get the cutters he could snip a hole in the wire at the front of the receiving cage and get out.

That would put him inside the fences and he could wade ashore before the shark would be able to get to him.

He took a breath and submerged himself and poked his extended fingers through the wire—shoved and strained them, not caring how badly he cut himself if he could only reach those clippers.

His taut fingers fell short of the tool by two inches.

The shark's perpendicular tail fanned the water and it glided forward toward the man's hand.

Robbins reared back, and the shark's pectorals spread as it drifted to a complete stop. It hung there, six feet from the wire, its dark striped back aglow with dapplings of refracted light cast from the sun on the water.

Robbins stood up and got his breath. All the barramunda, groper, salmon, trevally, and butterfish were thrashing wildly around him.

The water was now over his belt, and rising.

The shark made a sudden movement, skimming along the side of the cage. Robbins stood inside and watched it go—watched it make an abrupt turn around and slow to a halt.

For a moment the man and the shark stared at each other through the open gate of the cage.

Robbins threw himself into the water, making a frantic grab at the gate and shoving it closed just as the king-sized shark suddenly lunged at him.

The shark's mouth popped open and slammed shut at Robbins' hand as he snatched it back, and then it veered sharply to the right and its gleaming white belly rasped along the wire. It gave a quick flip of its mighty tail and shot off into the water.

The little fish swam around Robbins' legs as he waded through them to reach the front of the cage. Desperation was making him frantic.

He stared at the long narrow receiving entrance. It was just possible that he might be able to jam his body into it—but it was submerged and he was certain that he could never hold his breath long enough to wiggle himself through the chute.

In a little while the tide would rise over his head and over the mesh-roofed cage. He either had to get out or stay there and drown. But was the shark after him or was it after the trapped fish? And why did it have to be a tiger shark? One of the most infamous man-killers. Only a madman would risk going out bare-handed to face a tiger shark.

He plowed aimlessly through the swirling fish, first to one side of the cage, then to the other—trapped in his own cage, thinking how ironic his situation had become!

The sea kept coming in, bringing with it little riffles of white water. And now a southeast wind was starting. The wind would stir up the mud and sand in the bay and he wouldn't even be able to see what the shark was up to.

The tiger shark had completed its circle and was now cruising along the right side of the cage, gazing through the wire mesh at the trapped man and fish, its great jaw chewing at the water in a lateral motion as if speculating on the excellent meal that it hoped for.

It gave Robbins an idea. He had once observed the

keepers feed the sharks at Taronga Zoo in Sydney. Maybe he could distract the tiger's attention with some of his own fish; just long enough to let him get out of the cage and swim to the fence. . . .

He splashed through the water, chasing the caged fish, grabbing at their flashing oily bodies with both hands, and managed to catch a fat diamond-scaled mullet. The fish gave him a fierce struggle, but he was finally able to ease open the gate and pitch it outside. Sic'm, tiger!

But the mullet was a live fish and it had no intention of presenting itself to the voracious shark. It zipped across the coral and was gone. The myopic-eyed shark hadn't even noticed the mullet.

"Why did I throw all those dead fish away?" Robbins cursed. The dead fish couldn't escape. They would have made a perfect decoy. He couldn't save himself by crying over his mistakes.

This time he latched on to the tail of a king salmon and opened the gate and let the big active fish wriggle and squirm frenziedly until the shark definitely spotted it. Abrupt as sudden death the shark zoomed forward like a torpedo with its fanged mouth open.

Robbins, in panic, jerked backward and hauled the gate shut—forgetting that the scared salmon was still in his hand!

Robbins was thankful that the support stakes were firmly driven into the coral shelf. They and the tough wire mesh were all that separated him from a bloody death.

He waded to the front of the cage again, sick with discouragement and fear, and scanned the jungled shore that was so very close—only two hundred feet —yet so very very far away.

His desperate gaze searched the glittery bay. Empty. Forlornly void of life—except for that inexorable shark fin cutting back and forth, back and forth in the water. His fingers interlocked in the wire as he stared at the deserted bay and the inaccessible shore. And to think that he had been so pleased with himself for selecting such an isolated spot!

Suddenly his fear and frustration became too much to bear and he cried out for help. But his call was ineffectual against the immensity of the silent sea and the mute jungle. It was absorbed as easily as a whisper on a desert.

The sea splashed at his breast and he climbed up the wire until the top of his head bumped on the mesh over the cage. The late morning high tide was coming and he was running out of time. Soon now the cage would be submerged.

Which was worse—to drown in the cage or to be eaten alive by the shark?

A small wave slapped at his shoulder blades and he tried to cram himself a little higher on the wire. One of his bare feet brushed against the scoop which was leaning against the cage just below him. He thought about it. . . .

Would it work if he put the scoop over his head and shoulders and tried to swim to the fence in it?

He looked at the shark. The barrel-bodied brute was just taking another start at the cage. Its gaping mouth was a great tilted V, inset with hundreds of bright, jagged teeth.

No; he didn't have the stomach to attempt it. The shark would be bound to get him by the legs. Still, he should be able to do something with that scoop; had to, because it was his only implement.

Trying to feed the shark one fish at a time was no good; but suppose he fed the brute a whole batch at once, dumped out a big scoopload of fish that would burst apart like a bomb in the outer water?

It was worth a try. All he needed was to distract the shark's attention for a couple of minutes. He would actually settle for one minute if he could get it. Sixty precious seconds.

He dropped into the water, sucked a deep breath, submerged himself, and started snatching up the squirming slippery fish and jamming them into the scoop.

He worked methodically, urgently, popping to the surface every thirty seconds to catch his breath, and then submerging again and grabbing fish, every kind of fish, into the scoop, until their heads and tails and fins were sticking through the wire, razoring his clutching hands on their needlelike spines and fins, but not caring about the cuts because it was his life that was at stake.

Now the scoop was packed tight with the wriggling mass and he folded over the top ends so that none of the fish could slip out. His bare feet lacerating themselves on the coral, he dragged the balky scoop toward the gate, bobbing up twice to get his breath. He set the scoop against the gate and straightened up to locate the shark.

His time was very short now because the sea was up to his neck.

He spotted the shark. It was just turning away from the fence, knifing cleanly and swiftly through the water on another inspection tour of the cage. Robbins got his breath and sank down and started fumbling with the wire fastenings on the gate.

It looked as if the timing would be perfect. Just as the shark curved around the corner at the rear of the cage, he would dump out his scoopful of colorful fish and the shark would automatically go chomping after them.

The gate was unfastened. He reached for the scoop —and froze as he saw a second torpedolike shape streaking across the coral shelf, coming directly for the cage.

It was another shark!

It was a thirteen-foot saw shark and it was coming to join the tiger. Its three-foot-long swordlike snout was armed with spines along the sides, giving it the appearace of a large double-toothed saw, and Robbins knew that its peculiar teeth in its huge underslung jaw could grind a man into mincemeat.

The sight of the new shark was too much. His spirit sank and he was ready to give up. Against one shark he might have had a chance to escape, but what hope could he have with two of the huge fish after him?

The rising sea was splashing in his face. He climbed up the wire and clung there like a helpless sailor clinging to the ratlines on a sinking ship. Then he began to cry and curse. He knew it was a futile thing to do, but he couldn't seem to help it. His nerves were nearly un-raveled. He was going to drown in the cage, he knew it, and the realization was appalling.

Gasping and cursing, clinging to the wall of the cage with his head jammed against the mesh roof and with the sea splattering over his chin, he yelled and ranted at the two creatures who were going to cost him his life.

Suddenly he shut up, staring fixedly at the two active triangular fins.

The water around the gate was being lashed into a boiling foam as first the tiger, then the saw shark banged furiously against the wire, trying to get to the fish-packed scoop just inside the gate. In a moment they switched tactics and began to charge the cage together like a pair of battering rams. Soon the strained wire was bulging and bending and the support stakes threatened to snap at every head-on blow. The two carnivorous predators were completely hunger-crazed!

It was at that moment that Robbins began to reas-sert himself. He would not wait in the cage to drown like a craven rat. If he had to die, then he would leave the world fighting. He would go out and meet the two killers on their own ground: in the sea.

"You want the scoop, do you?" he yelled at them. "All right, I'll give it to you!"

He sucked a breath and dropped into the water, fumbled for the gate fastenings with one hand and grabbed the scoop with the other. And in that last mad instant he had a brainstorm. He wouldn't open the wire ends on the scoop and let the flurry of fish scatter. . . .

I'll feed the beggars whole hog, he thought.

He shoved open the gate and yelled *Blaaah!* under-water in a great belch of activated bubbles. Startled, both sharks made a laterally compressed sweep with their big tails and shot off at right angles—but not far. They slowed with their fanlike pectorals, back-rolling their eyes.

With a tremendous heave, Robbins propelled the heavy fish-packed scoop through the gate and went up to get his breath.

The tiger shark was cruising in a tight circle, its port eye extended, vicious. It saw the scoop first and instantly bolted toward it, unslinging its shopping-bag mouth and snapping its jaw on the prize. With a silvery rush the saw shark flashed in and made a sideswipe grab at the scoop with its jagged maw, and got it, and then tried to tail-hitch itself across the coral shelf to make off with it, but the outraged tiger was right on the saw's flank and it snatched the scoop back, and then first one had it, then the other, both slashing wire and fish and each other with their jaws.

Finally they both dropped the scoop and turned directly on each other. Twisting and thrashing through long distorted streaks of crimson, they spun around and around in the turquoise water like a pair of cat-erine wheels spurting off scarlet fireworks.

All this time Robbins was clinging to the cage and gasping for air with his mouth glued to the wire mesh roof, sucking a breath only in the shallow hollow between the choppy waves as they splashed over his head —waiting, praying, for the sharks to get farther out on the reef and give him a chance to make a bolt for it. But they were too engaged in fighting each other for either one of them to attempt to escape with the scoop; and though they were still dangerously close to the cage, Robbins knew that his time was now. He had no choice. He couldn't hold on to the wire a moment longer; already he was gulping more saltwater than air.

Half choking, he let go and swam down through the gate, came to the surface and turned and grabbed for the outside wire and scrabbled up on the sagging roof of the cage. He paused for a moment, catching his breath and looking around for the sharks.

Ten yards off in the water a widening splotch of blood glittered in the morning sun. It was shattered by a sudden roil of foam as a splayed tail leaped up and slammed the surface. Those thirty feet were probably the only margin of safety he was going to get.

He crawled over to the south fence, to the point where it hinged on the funnel mouth of the receiving cage, and started to climb along its wobbly top. It was barely submerged in the backwash water, and for that reason it wouldn't do him any good to get inside the Y-shaped pen, because each time a shore-bound wave topped the wire it carried enough water to lift a shark over the fence.

He inched along frantically, the strained wire sagging and wig-wagging under him, lacerating the insides of his thighs and buttocks painfully, with each incoming comber rolling over his head; and when he had covered only eighty feet of the two-hundred-foot-long fence, he glanced back and gave a shocked gasp.

The saw shark had the torn scoop in its greedy

mouth and was trying to run away with it. But the great brute was coming straight for the fence with the furious tiger shark right on its tail!

The shortsighted saw shark didn't see the submerged fence until it was too late, and it slammed into the wire only six feet behind the crouching man. It dropped the battered scoop, and just then a fat comber rolled over Robbins and the fence, and its impetus carried the oncoming tiger shark into the Y-shaped pen.

The saw shark on one side, the tiger shark on the other, and Robbins straddling the wobbly submerged fence between them!

He kept crawling along the giving wire. There was nothing else he could do! Fearfully, he glanced over his right shoulder, then over his left. The tiger was banging its blunt snout against the fence, trying to get at the scoop on the other side; the saw shark had the scoop, but it quickly learned that the thing was empty.

The saw shark hung for a moment in the bright green water and stared at Robbins. Its eyes seemed to bulge with sudden recognition, and it closed its pectorals and bolted forward.

Robbins piled over the fence—on the side with the tiger shark.

Please God, he prayed, keep it worrying after that scoop.

One hundred feet to go. The saw shark threw himself *wham* against the wire as Robbins backfinned underwater. Then the saw veered off, one yard from his face, and the compression from its big tail spun Robbins half around. He scrambled back onto the fence and started pulling himself along the wire as the saw shark commenced a wide banking turn to come after him again.

He threw a hurried look over his shoulder. The tiger shark was wild now with all the blood scent in the water and seemed to be completely out of its mind. It was still furiously bumping against the wire, trying to get to that empty fish scoop.

The persistent saw shark was coming again—coming in the breast of a big shorebound wave. Robbins sucked air and swung off the fence as the wave rolled over his head, and for one blurry moment he saw the rising saw's snout lunge into an upward tilt, and saw the gleam of the great white belly as the brute washed right over his jackknifing body.

His clutching hands dragged his body up to the wire and he climbed the fence, over the top, and plunged down on the other side. With only his head above water and gasping for air, he hauled himself hand-over-hand along the outside of the wire.

He knew he had won.

Both of the sharks were now inside the pen and the incoming sea would keep them there until he could reach the shore. The saw shark dogged him right into the surf, baffled and frustrated by the wire that wouldn't let it get to the man. Finally, out of its element in the shallow water, it gave up and turned away to go seek something else to eat.

Robbins, worn out, crawled from the water and into the safety of the shore and lay down on the warm sand. All around him flowed the sunny morning sea breeze, and the silence.

9 SAVAGE GROUND

In the first cold glow of dawn the Japanese sea-man Koji Ahara swam across a broad coral shelf for the small jungled island that rose up on a steep beach of white sand. Beneath him, and for thousands of miles around, lay a stupendous mountain of coral, betrayed only by the dozens of little cays and out-croppings. The Great Barrier Reef of Australia.

The tide was ebbing and there was only half a fathom of water covering the shelf. The demolition sack that hung from Ahara's neck brushed the top of a squat mushroom coral, and he looked down with his face mask, startled, and pulled it to his chest.

Now that he was about to leave the sea to walk on dry land, he was suddenly very conscious of the under-water demolition sack. There might be some Aussies patrolling the barrier reef, and if they caught him with high explosives. . . .

A coral pit opened below him. He checked his progress, peering down through the dawn-illuminated water. Obviously when the tide receded and the coral shelf lay bare, this pit would become a sheltered tide-pool, two fathoms deep. He jacknifed to the bottom and concealed the demolition sack behind a giant staghorn. Reaching carefully—he was afraid of coral poisoning—he snapped a coral pad from the living wall and placed it over the sack.

He felt better as he continued toward the island. All he had to do now was wait to be picked up.

It was the middle of 1944 and the war in the Coral Sea was going very badly for the Japanese. They had lost the Solomon Islands and the Bismarck Archipelago, and now the combined Allied American and Australian forces were mopping up the Imperial Army on New Guinea. Without air or sea support, the beleaguered Japanese had been fighting doggedly and hopelessly from one end of the great island to the other.

To cinch the inevitable conclusion of the battle the Australians had been landing more and more troops on the coast of Papua—and Ahara had been given the unenviable job of trying to intercept and destroy one of the Papua-bound troopships.

Through secret information the Japanese command knew the ship was scheduled to come up the inside of the Great Barrier Reef to cross the Torres Straits, and they had selected one of their newly trained underwater demolition men to be waiting for the ship off Cape York.

But everything had gone wrong. The Japanese had carried Ahara out to sea three hours before dawn, in a high-powered launch, and they had easily located the ponderous troopship carefully feeling its way through the coral-toothed water in the dark. And then they had discovered that the big ship had a gunboat escort.

"Get into the water quickly, Ahara!" an officer had ordered the young Japanese. "After you have set the charge against the ship's hull, swim to Riga Cay. We will pick you up in the morning."

The Aussie gunboat had spotted the launch and she started to fire at it with her forward gun. The first shell squirted a tall column of water just off the launch's port quarter, and the officer began to scream at Ahara.

"Jump, Ahara! Jump! We have to get away!"

Stunned by the abrupt and clamorous action, Ahara had rolled over the rail, had hit the turbulent water, and sunk into throbbing blackness.

The Japanese had not known about the gunboat, which promptly gave chase to the skittering launch. Worse than that, now that the troopship had been warned of an approaching enemy, it hastily turned off course. And within five minutes Ahara had found himself treading water all alone in the dark channel, with the useless demolition sack hanging from his neck.

Ahara floated into the beach, belly-down, pulled himself heavily onto the sand, shoved up the face mask, and looked along the empty length of the jungled shore. A soft moan reached him above the grumble of the surf. He listened. They had told him the cay was uninhabited.

The rush and wash of the surf impaired his hearing. He shrugged and stood up, stripped the rubber fins from his feet. It was probably just his ears, still full of sea-sound. Yes, that was all. It was nothing.

The eastern horizon began to turn as the sun rose. With the light Ahara suddenly felt conspicuous and vulnerable on the open beach.

It would be best to seek cover in the jungle, as the launch might not come for two or three hours.

An instinctive sense of danger struck him without warning, and he spun about on the sand.

Legions of quarter-sized soldier crabs were marching across the shimmering flats. Ahara snatched up his fins and stepped back quickly. He watched the thousands—millions, he thought, of glistening creatures march across the sand. Their fat bodies and spidery legs held him with a sickening fascination. Somewhere in his memory a sentence he had read in his youth repeated itself in his mind: All crabs are flesh-eaters.

With a wave of revulsion, he turned and ran for the jungle. When he looked back the crabs were gone— vanished, as though they had never existed.

Just within the fringe of the foliage, Ahara sat in the weeds with his back against a giant pisonia tree. When he glanced at his hands he found them wrinkled and grayish from the long time spent in the sea. He was hungry, and very thirsty.

He closed his eyes. He'd had a bad time out there in the water. After he'd lost the troopship he'd discovered that the lung-pack was not functioning correctly. Finally he had jettisoned it. Then for a long time he hadn't been able to find the Riga Cay. He didn't know why he had hung onto the demolition sack. He knew it wasn't going to be used. But somehow it didn't seem expendable.

He sighed wearily and leaned his head back against

the tree trunk. He was only eighteen and this was his first active mission. He had been well trained in the use of underwater equipment and demolitions, but the thing that now disturbed him was that no one had taught him how to exist on a small coral island.

He studied the horizon, judging the time at five thirty, wishing that he could grab time in his hand and force it ahead. What if they didn't come for him until nine or ten in the morning? He was too impatient to sit still.

He stood up and began to wander through the weeds and sand. Maybe he could find a spring to drink from. But he doubted it. What he needed was a rain shower. He stared moodily downward as he walked, and though he saw the ground crumble beneath his feet, it happened too abruptly to register a warning in his mind. He plunged knee-deep into a shallow pit. He gasped with pain, his left ankle badly wrenched. Some creature had evidently honeycombed the ground, burrowing out a nest.

He reached above his head for a sturdy-looking pisonia branch to pull himself up by. It snapped like a matchstick, flinging him into the sand again. He stared at the brittle branch, feeling a little silly. But he realized that these two minor incidents served as a warning.

He had come ashore on a strange land that he knew nothing about. The Great Barrier Reef was not a playground for the inexperienced. Every step might lead to a pitfall; thick trees snapped under moderate weight; wild creatures lurked in the jungled growth; and out on the coral shelf that beckoned like a fabulous jeweled treasure, the danger was manifold.

Poisonous coral, glass-sharp, ready to crumble without warning; this sea plant was poisonous, that one was not, and who could tell the difference? The same with the fish. Voracious sharks and lurking moray eels, and stingrays drifting in the shallows; and everywhere a needlelike spine on the back of a hidden fish which could pierce a hand or foot.

He returned to the beach and looked at the sea. In the distance the shape of Queensland loomed in the sky, sixteen miles from the cay. Sixteen miles . . . He looked away. The coral shelf was bare now in a riot of color. The tidepools stained the reef like turquoise cups.

He glanced at the sun every two or three minutes now. It must be almost eight A.M. He went out on the reef a few yards and looked at the sea. Empty.

He returned to the beach and began walking around the island. He made a complete tour, twice, then flung himself down on the warm sand and closed his eyes. He felt tired, dizzy from sun and glare, hunger and worry; raw and tense and thirsty.

What was delaying them? It was noon. Before, when he had had an appointed hour to await, he had remained comparatively calm; but now, with no definite time alloted, he started to panic. His thirst had to be appeased. If he could catch a fish he could drink its lymph juices.

Under a sun of incandescent white, he limped across the shelf. A coral lily crumpled underfoot, pitching him into a deep pool. Something like a pulsating umbrella hung blurred before his eyes, rainbow-hued and jellied. It was a Portuguese man-of-war. Didn't their touch have a serious numbing effect? At any rate, how could you eat one? He turned away, looking deeper into the pool. Among the green algae, lumpy tiger coral and the hard coralline purple cement, lay a giant tridacna—crooked valves open, exposing its emerald-green maw as it emitted a steady stream of water from a siphon about the size of a firehose.

He had heard they were man-killers. They catch a diver in their strong jaws and hold him until he drowns.

He pulled himself over the edge of the pool, shoving up his face mask. He splashed across a broad two-inch-deep pool studded with flat lavender coralheads, searching for anything alive for his sustenance. In the slimy crevice he found a battered pail.

With the pail in his hand some of his confidence returned. Now he could catch fish.

He went after a large crab; the creature scuttled sideways and dropped out of sight into a pool. Ahara told himself, "I'll catch something in a minute." But the minute passed and after that he forgot about time.

Sweating under the white glare of the afternoon, he discovered a solitary parrot fish in a narrow, shallow pool. He waded in cautiously, the pail between his hands. The parrot fish stirred, flipped its fin, and disappeared over the far end of the pool. He went after it. The fish spun a tight circle and darted between his legs. Ahara scooped frantically, lost his balance, and sprawled headlong into the water.

Breathing heavily, he began to bail out the pool. He worked furiously, stopping only once when he scraped his knuckles on the poisonous coral. He worked for a long time before he realized that the water level wasn't dropping. Then he discovered a crevice in the coral leading to an adjoining pool. He plugged the gap with a leathery sea plant and resumed bailing.

He worked carefully now, striving to be calm, but his heart pounded in his chest and his hands were trembling. After twenty minutes of labor the pool was dry. But the fish was gone.

He waded over to the next pool. The mottled green parrot hung drowsily in the clear water. It had escaped through the crevice before he'd plugged it. The next pool would take a week to bail.

Leaving the coral shelf, he threw himself on the beach. Why didn't they come for him? Why? He sat up after a moment and scanned the empty sea. He felt forgotten. A shadow of fear expanded in his mind. Would they leave him here?

Alone on the mightiest coral structure on earth, he began to understand the true meaning of survival. In the end it came down to each man on his own, just as it had been in the beginning of time; basic man against the primal elements.

He worked doggedly through the long afternoon, chasing fish from pool to pool, without hope, like an automaton. He knew he needed sleep, perhaps more than food, but his hunger and thirst were so great he couldn't stop. Finally the light waned, and when he looked up he saw the sun sinking near the horizon. The twilight flood began, and soon he was thrashing knee-deep across the submerged shelf.

"While there's light, there's hope," he thought. He

waded ashore to get his fins. He fashioned a crude wooden spear with his sheath knife.

He returned to the water and floated on the surface. It was like a cool bed. He drifted over a sunken vault, alive with wavering sea anemones. He hungrily eyed a small clownfish who watched him impassively from its protective home among the anemones' poisonous tentacles. It was useless to chase the fish which required but a split second to dart to distant safety.

He followed a dense school of trevally over the edge of the outer reef and into deeper water. With a spurt of action they were gone, and Ahara hung alone in the sea. He turned and started back for the ledge.

Then he spotted a fat sea cucumber—the trepang —and he reached for it thankfully. The ugly sausage-shaped animal was a meal.

On the shelf again, he stood upright in the waist-high water to get his breath. He was so tired that his eye centered on the gliding heterocercal fin for a second before its significance registered in his mind. Suddenly he was wide awake and underwater again, his face toward the distant cay. A six-foot bronze whaler shark stood clearly defined in the translucent water.

Ahara had stayed out too long. During the flood tide, hunting sharks venture across the reefs to feed. He knew that more than a hundred species of shark infested the Coral Sea, and that only a few of them were considered man-eaters. The trouble was, he didn't know one from another.

Clutching the feeble spear and the sticky trepang, he circled away from the giant fish and headed for a tall bush coral with some vague idea of hiding. He looked back. The shark was gliding effortlessly behind his fins. Frantically he kicked about in a half-circle, bringing his legs under and behind. The shark nosed in closer, its myopic eyes watchful, searching.

Ahara dropped the trepang and grabbed the spear in both hands. The shark seemed more curious than dangerous, but at such close range Ahara couldn't afford to take chances. He pricked the shark's blunt snout with the spear point.

Instantly he was struck by the backwash of the shark's swirling flight. He turned and finned wildly for the beach. It was only as he passed the hole with the demolition sack that he remembered the sea cucumber. But it was too late. He didn't have the nerve to return for it.

In the late evening he reentered the jungle and heard again the moaning that had startled him earlier. It was coming from the trees: an unearthly series of howls, groans, and sighs. He walked carefully, keeping his eyes on the twisted growth above, sensing uneasily that a man could go mad from listening to too much of that noise.

He jumped at the sound of a whirring beneath his feet and a flash of feathers before his eyes. The moaning stopped. A muttonbird fled off into the jungle.

Ahara on his knees stalked the muttonbirds as a cat stalks a sparrow. The coral cut on his knuckles was giving him pain, but the pain of hunger was greater.

Once he crawled upon a bird that must have been asleep; but the light was poor and he didn't see it till it shot up in his face. He lunged forward, clutching with both hands and sprawled in the sand with two small tail-feathers in his fingers.

He stood up finally and placed his hands over his ears and screamed and howled back at the raucous birds. Then he turned back to the beach and threw himself on the sand.

He looked at the channel, toward the continent that was screened by the night. Sixteen miles. He shook his head. He had to have food and drink.

Something was coming from the water to the edge of the surf—long, glistening and black, like a giant log being pushed ashore end first by the tide. Ahara crouched and watched. Another skin diver? But some inner sense of apprehension warned him that it was nothing human. Then, as the thing kept coming from the water, he knew for certain that it was not.

The monster sprawled bulkily on the dark sand and emitted a sort of wheezing hiss. Then it began to waddle inland.

Ahara jumped and ran for the jungle. It was the last thing he would have thought of, a danger he hadn't counted on—a seagoing crocodile from the mangrove estuaries of Cape York. The sea was no barrier for them; they were at home in saltwater as well as fresh water. Their length frequently exceeded thirty feet, which gave them confidence over any enemy. And, like the tiger, they were reputed to have a yen for human flesh.

Ahara stopped beneath a twisted pisonia, glanced over his shoulder—and his foot pushed through the roof of a muttonbird nest. He toppled sideways, making a smash in the brittle thicket. The giant crocodile lifted its heavy snout, paused questioningly, then moved toward him, its webbed feet making tracks in the sand.

Ahara knew he would rather die of hunger and thirst than be caught in those crushing jaws. He ran blindly into the jungle.

A pisonia trunk sprang before his face and he collided head on. He staggered backward and heard the peculiar hiss behind him.

He stared at the savage head, at the pitted skin, the large keeled bony scutes. The crocodile opened its elongated jaws, showing its fearsome pointed pillars of ivory in the moonlight, and rushed him.

Ahara sidestepped and ran into the bush. Before him loomed a pandanus tree. That was safety; it would support his weight. He scrambled up to the high branches and secured himself in a fork. Below, in the darkness, he could hear the scurry and grunt of the crocodile. He closed his eyes and leaned his forehead against the bark.

All around him the moan and sigh and howl of the muttonbirds mingled with the rumble of the sea. He dozed fitfully, waking with starts and with pain.

When the new day broke and the muttonbirds ceased their moans and winged out to sea, he left the tree. He was certain now that the launch wasn't coming for him In fact, he doubted if they had ever intended to rescue him. They had probably considered him an expendable on a suicide mission.

He accepted the realization calmly now. He needed food and drink. Only after these necessities could he take the next step toward survival. Sixteen miles. . . .

He circled the cay to see if the crocodile was still there, but the saurian had vanished with the dawn. Then he began to dig into the nests of the muttonbirds for their eggs. He knew what had defeated him the previous day: he had acted in desperation. And that was the quickest way to be defeated.

The eggs he uncovered he ate raw. Next, he reclaimed his pail and went out on the bare coral shelf. He spotted a school of parrot fish at the head of a line of shallow pools, and he circled them in knee-deep water and began to press shoreward. The school scurried into the shallows and he hurried after them, stepping high in the water and around the coral patches. When they endeavored to turn off and seek deeper water, he shouted and beat the bottom of the pail, racing ahead to cut off their line of retreat.

Gradually he closed them into a narrow pool. The fish bunched under the overhang of a coralhead. Ahara scooped up a four-pounder that was so fatigued it hardly bothered to make an escape.

He stabbed the glistening body with his knife, tilted back his head and squeezed the lymphatic juice of the fish into his mouth. It was oily, with a trace of blood, but free of salt. He placed the carcass on the coral and caught three more. After he had drained them dry, he cut them into strips and ate them raw.

When he had finished eating, he stood up and looked at the land ahead of him. If he was going to do it, then it must be done now. Sixteen miles to Queensland.

Beyond the reef the sea was like watered silk, blue

and glossy, silent except for the sigh of the ocean. At the reef's outer edge small waterfalls, rushing to catch the tide, were continually appearing and vanishing. Ahara pulled on his fins and adjusted his mask.

He didn't consider the possible failure or success of this venture. It was simply something that had to be done. He waited until the tide flooded over his ankles, and he stepped off the ledge.

As the tips of his fins touched the sandy bottom of the sea, he reached for a rough protrusion to hold himself. Even as he snatched back his hand he knew it was too late. Stonefish—the perfect counterpart of a piece of weathered coral. The fish's thirteen needle-sharp spines bristled erect, and Ahara felt the hypodermic-like jab in his little finger.

He turned away, hugging the burning hand to his breast. It was impossible to try to reach the mainland now, with the overpowering pain that was searing through his body. He couldn't believe it had happened. After all he had been through, an insignificant fish with a weapon no larger than a darning needle had brought him down.

He broke the surface and pulled himself over the edge of the shelf. He stumbled toward the lonely cay.

The pain was unbearable. All through the long day he rolled and thrashed on the sand. And later—in delirium—he alternately threw himself into the shallows and went running off blindly through the jungle. Then, in the night, he joined the muttonbird chorus and wailed his torment.

At midnight he found himself staggering on the

empty beach. He looked at the sea, at the eternal stretch and glimmer and wash. Then he remembered the demolition sack.

He hobbled across the flooded reef and sank into the inky tide pool where he had hidden the sack. He opened the sack and set the timing fuse. Then he went thrashing back to the beach.

He had not quite reached the shelter of the jungle when the submerged shelf exploded. The charge shot a tall column of water and white flame high into the dark sky, and the roar and blast sent him sprawling in the sand. He lay with his face buried in his arms as bits of metal, wood, fish, and great jets of water rained down on him.

When it was dawn again and he was sitting on the sand staring vacantly at the sea, he thought perhaps he might die that day, but he no longer had the energy left to do anything about it. His eyes centered on a small moving object, and for a moment he simply stared stupidly at the boat that was chopping evenly toward the cay.

At once, he was on his feet and yelling hoarsely. The launch! Was it possible?

But it wasn't the launch. It was an Australian gunboat.

Ahara didn't care. He splashed across the coral shelf, waving his good arm at the Aussies. They glided along the edge of the submerged shelf, all of them watching Ahara wade out to them. A couple of seamen hooked him aboard, taking care of his swollen arm, and helped him aft.

"Say, mate," one of them said to him. "You make that explosion out 'ere last night?"

Ahara didn't understand English, and he made no reply. He wasn't up to talking anyhow. The boat was moving out and he looked back at the cay. He had been maroroned there for only two days, yet it had seemed like a lifetime. Now he was leaving it to become a prisoner, and he was thankful.

10 TO TAKE A STEP

The storm that raged out of the sea and over the Andes in the winter of 1930 was now one week past and the two airmail pilots, Saint Exupéry and Deley, had been ransacking the icy mountains for five days, searching for a comrade who had gone down in the snowy maelstrom.

There were only two planes to explore a vast wilderness that called for ten squadrons to do the job correctly. Scouring back and forth across the endless cloudy range, slipping in and out of the giant pillars of the Cordilleras—looking for the proverbial needle in the haystack.

It was hopeless. They both knew it. They landed at Santiago and Saint Exupéry tried to form a rescue party among the Chilean natives. They told him no, not for any price.

"We would surely die," they said. "The Andes never gives up a man in winter."

The Chilean officers told them the same thing. "Even if your comrade survived the landing, he cannot have survived the nights," they said. "Night in those passes changes a man into ice."

Exupéry and Deley knew it was true, and Exupéry said, "That last time we went up, I felt it was more of a tribute than a search. As if I were sitting up with his body—like in the silence of a cathedral of snow."

Deley nodded, staring at the ground. "Then that's that," he said. "Guillaumet is gone . . . and he was the best of us."

The storm that had caught Guillaumet had brought fifteen feet of snow in forty-eight hours down on the Chilean hills and had sent most of the mail pilots scuttling back to their starting points.

But Guillaumet was a pioneer pilot, one of those who had opened up the night flights over the Andes in the late 1920's, searching out the gaps in the great Cordilleras which loomed more than 20,000 feet into the air—searching for them in a flimsy one-seater biplane whose top ceiling was 16,000 feet.

Storms didn't frighten him. He respected them and even liked them. He took off in the hope of finding a rift in the blustering sky, an opening in the narrow walls of some rocky corridor. He found it a little to the south and climbed to 20,000, placing the ceiling of clouds 2,000 feet below the bottom of his plane, and set his course for Argentina.

The down currents above the clouds were tricky. They appeared to be absolutely stationary simply because in that high altitude they never stopped flowing. Nothing shook or rattled, the engine was running smoothly, the five tons of metal around him were vibrating quietly—but the plane seemed to be sinking.

He kicked the rudder bar and jockeyed for altitude. Still something was queer. He seemed to be losing speed and the controls felt loose in his gloved hands. He ducked his head into the cockpit. The red light glowed faintly on the dials. He could barely see the gyroscope and manometers.

He let her drift to the right, glancing around at the high peaks with their streaming snow, off which the wind rebounded as from a springboard. But he was still dropping.

The stars went out. The wall of clouds reared high over the tattered crags and the wind-driven sleet came in broad sheets against the peaks. The tough little plane flew through this, and slid quickly and sickeningly down over a great empty cavern beyond, rocking, tilting, slithering about helplessly.

Guillaumet was caught and he knew it; he dropped the controls and grabbed his seat for fear of being flung out of the cockpit. The jolts were so violent that the leather harness cut his shoulders and threatened to snap.

The light was dimming and he snapped on the flying light to see if he could spot a wing, but he couldn't. All he saw was the flame from the exhaust clinging to the motor like a spray of witch-fire.

The wind bowled him over and he dropped down to ten feet. Then he spotted a dark horizontal blot that helped him right the ship. He recognized it. Laguna Diamante, a lake that lay at the bottom of a funnel-shaped cluster of mountains.

He was out of the clouds but still blinded by the

whirling snow, and he had to cling to the lake to keep from piling into the face of one of the bleached white mountains surrounding him. Around and around he banked like a fly caught in a bottle, gliding slantwise just inside those great earthen giants which rose above, until he ran out of fuel.

He launched a landing flare. It sputtered and spun and illuminated a broad snowfield one hundred and fifty feet below He put the controls forward, corrected the gliding angle, and went down.

The earth was like a great white bed and he knew it would be a crash landing and he shoved his goggles over his eyes. The landing gear sliced the snow and the ship cut along like a plow.

A lurch—a violent jerk—a whiplash through his body, and the plane nosed in and went right over on her prop. Guillaumet hung in suspended animation upside down, waiting apprehensively.

He dragged himself clear of the wreck and stood up. The wind flattened him in the snow. Then he crawled back under the cockpit and dug out a shelter in the snow, pulled a pile of mail sacks around him, and huddled shivering in his little nest.

He looked at the pile of letters which he had risked his life to deliver. Bills and bank statements and postcards saying, Wish you were here. He wished he could be there—anywhere except where he was.

He took stock of his situation. It was freezing. He was freezing. He was clad in his full-length Sidcott and that was some help. So were his gloves and boots. He had a knife and watch and compass, and that was it. He rather doubted that anyone would find the wreck from the air, and even if he was spotted no one would be crazy enough to try to rescue him on foot.

"So," he decided, "if they won't come to me, I'll go to them."

He would walk out—try to.

"I'm dead if I stay here," he thought. "I might as well die trying to live."

The storm tore at the Andes for two days and then blew itself out and Guillaumet crawled from his fox-hole and started to walk. It was a short walk that soon became a climb, a crawl, an inchwormlike method of motion.

The mighty Andes call for professional moun-taineers with all their scaling paraphernalia; and there was Guillaumet without ropes or pitons or an ice-ax, scaling snow-rotten cols 15,000 feet in the frosted air without provisions.

All around him the lonely mountains rose into the milky sky. His descent through them was slow and treacherous because their water-saturated skins were in a state of decomposition. They shed ice, snow, water, and were subject to abrupt and furious avalanches.

The rock crumbled under his frozen fingers and raw knees, and the wind swept around the jagged corners and ice buttresses and struck at him with sledgehammer blows, roaring and whimpering and clawing at his clothes.

By the end of the first day his hands and knees were skinned bare and bleeding, and he had to stop every two or three hours to cut his boots open a bit more to give his swollen feet room.

"Thank God my socks stretch," he thought.

The temperature was twenty degrees below zero. When the burning in his throat became too intense he melted snow in his mouth and used it for water, or for fuel. He would have given anything for one chocolate bar.

Loss of blood and strength and even reason began to play tricks on his memory. It was the second night when he suddenly realized that during one of his rest periods to massage his puffy feet, he had left his watch behind on a rock.

"Must be careful," he thought dully. "Must keep a clear head."

It wasn't easy. His hunger and pain and utter exhaustion were turning him into a plodding automaton. . . .

He went forward, upward, downward with the obstinacy of an ant, avoiding deep chasms, traversing great sloping snowfields, scrabbling over enormous glacierlike mounds, picking himself stubbornly up after each fall, retracing his steps to get around some balky obstacle that reared in his path like a snow-clad troll.

Each time he backtracked he saw his own footprints coming toward him in the snow—one step after another, as if some abominable snowman had recently passed this way dragging himself homeward to the misty people of the snow.

Suddenly all those quiet-looking peaks and snowcaps and toothy crags seemed to come to life, heaving up and leaning in around him. His fagged brain reeled and he wondered if he was lost. He was too punch-drunk to remember that he had a compass.

The worse part was he had to keep in constant motion. Otherwise his blood would freeze and his brain would blank out and he would drop into a sleep that would whisk him into a frozen eternity.

Two nights and two days now, without sleep, always moving, knowing that even an innocent moment's sleep meant death. When an ankle turned or a hand slipped and he went down, he was up again in an instant, sensing that just a second too long in the soft snow would turn him to stone.

The cold was petrifying him by degrees and he had to pay an agonizing price in pain each time he paused for a rest and then had to get up and revivify his frozen muscles.

He trudged on, scaling the shark-toothed ridges, crawling the glassy faces of nearly vertical walls, urging himself on with the thought:

"What I am going through, no animal would go through."

The third day was very bad.

After three days of snow-crawling, all he could think about was sleep. His longing for it was greater than hunger or thirst. His harassed mind began to rationalize.

What was death, after all? Nothing but an inevitable fact. From the very moment of his birth he had started out on the inexorable road to death, and now it was here.

"What does it really matter," he asked, "whether I accept it here and now in this wilderness, or stall it off for another thirty years and then face it in a sickbed in France or some other place?"

He couldn't see that it actually mattered, and he started to let himself go, to sink deep into the feathery comfort of the snow. . . .

He saw his wife's face as a vague image with a stricken expression, and he thought, "If she still believes I am alive, she must believe that I am on my feet." Then he thought, "And all the pilots think I am on my feet They have faith in me. So I will go on."

He crawled on, pausing only to cut open his boots from time to time to relieve his swelling and freezing feet. But the pain of his hands and feet became almost too much for him and he had to force himself not to think, to ignore pain.

He tried to think about a movie he had seen. Then he put his mind on some book he had read.

"That's no good," he said. "Planes and pilots and death aren't the answer. Think of something else." But nothing worked. No matter what book or film he reviewed, it went through his mind like lightning and he would be back where he was—in the snow.

He put his mind on other things. . . .

At one time he had surveyed the Casablanca-Dakar line across the parched territory roved by the savage tribes of the Sahara. He thought about those romantic and violent times and he laughed to himself and struggled on. He was a little mad.

He stumbled along a ridge which belonged to a

mountain that millions of years ago was created by some earth cataclysm. It was serrated and gullied by erosion, its face dented and flattened and stained like a darkly gleaming death's head staring and sneering at the puny world of men.

But in his sudden energy of madness, Guillaumet laughed at it. He would take it as he had taken all the rest. He felt exhilarated.

Every mountain has its own peculiarities, its special tricks and startling surprises. And that is the thing that kills mountainers. And Guillaumet was no mountaineer.

It was comparatively easy at first, a matter of finding the right handhold, then foothold, then left and lower handhold and left and lower foothold, and then down and groping, finger-searching with the right hand again.

He went down the tilted face with arms and legs extended, like a spider on a wall. The misty bottom of the gorge beneath him seemed miles away and he had to stop looking down. The void was too immense.

He was clinging to a bulging protrusion, a bump of craggy old rock like a brow overhanging a sunken, noseless face—a gigantic brow sixty or seventy feet in diameter. To descend it would be like setting a ladder against a wall and trying to climb down the underside of the rungs.

He had no choice. He had to try. One thing only was in his favor—the composition of the rock was that of old wrinkled scar strata, rotten with cracks and fissures for his hands and feet. He started down. The gentle swell of the bulge swung under him and he took one quick glance below. A great empty space yawned under him and he looked away.

He realized that his progress was lagging. He was beginning to feel the down-drag more and more. His arms were aching, his legs too, and he was having trouble getting his breath. He had completely lost his sense of exhilaration.

"It's hopeless," he told himself. "This is the end. Let go."

But his fingers wouldn't open. They clung to the rock with tenacity as if his mind shut off this means of escape through self-destruction.

He sucked his breath and bared his teeth like a trapped animal preparing to bite. He inched his left hand down until it joined in the same slot with his right, and at the same time his right foot slipped from its tense position and gravity swung him away from the bulge and his entire body was attached to the mountain by only the eight fingers of his two hands.

He hung on, kicking with his right foot, toe-scratching for a grip that would swing his body inward again.

He felt the toe of his boot snub on something and it caught. He stalled, afraid to move any limb or muscle of his body. But he had to make the decisive move which would either be the beginning of the end, or the continuation of the struggle.

Hanging by a foot and a hand he reached down with his other hand and started clawing blindly at anything, everything, for a grip, and found one, his fingers biting into it like teeth, and took most of the weight with that hand as the other hand went after it and below it and found a fissure of its own.

Painfully he lowered himself onto a rocky shelf. Night was just closing over the brooding peaks. Guillaumet went on.

He slipped and fell flat on his face in the snow at dawn, and it was right at that precise moment that he knew his body was through. His arms and legs and fingers and toes simply couldn't take any more punishment.

Sleep was all that mattered. He simply had to close his eyes to shut out the nightmare world of crags and snow and ice. He snuggled in the snow like a weary man settling into a feather mattress. It felt very good, wonderful, and odd that it seemed so warm. . . .

He thought of his wife again. She would be penniless if she couldn't collect the insurance, and by law, when a man vanishes, his legal death is postponed for four years. "She won't get a cent for four years," he thought, "unless they find my body."

He was lying on a sloping snowfield and he knew that his body would be washed down with the slush when summer came—down into one of the thousands of deep crevasses where no one would ever find it. He raised his head and saw a broad rock jutting out of the snow some fifty yards away

"If I get up," he thought, "I may be able to reach it. And if I can prop myself up against the rock, they'll find me there next summer."

He reached the rock—and went on past it. Now

that he was on his feet again and moving it would be silly to stop. Maybe he could find a better rock to die upon farther below.

He trudged mechanically through the fourth day, from rock to rock, telling himself he was looking for the proper place to die, thinking, the spot where a man dies is very important. But he could no longer remember exactly why it was so important. In fact, he no longer seemed to be able to remember anything. His memory was playing tricks again.

It took him a long time to realize that every time he stopped to cut open his boots he forgot something. First it was a glove. He had put it down in front of him and had forgotten to pick it up. The next time it was his knife. Then his compass. At every pause he had stupidly stripped himself of something vitally important.

He was becoming his own enemy.

All the signs were against him. His fingers would no longer work. He couldn't feel his own feet. The skin on his face felt like a crust of rock. His vision was turning splotchy. And there was his heart. . . .

He didn't know what to do. He thought, "If it hesitates a moment too long, I drop." Never in his life had he listened to a cranky motor as carefully as he listened to his heart.

On the fifth day he was far below the snowline and he found nameless green growths on the scaly boulders. He put them in his mouth and chewed and swallowed them. He was willing to put nearly anything except ice inside his stomach.

That day he saw the shelving hills footing the

Argentine plains. He would have liked to run, but his feet would not allow it. He was barely hobbling. He paused for a moment to stare at the great spread of noon plains. They seemed remote and detached from his lofty position, but he knew it was only an illusion.

He took a heavy step and started the last part of his ordeal, coming back down into the world and among people.

The workers pruning the vineyards saw the strange emaciated creature shuffling toward them like a mechanical man, and they were struck with awe. They looked at his swollen stiffened hands and his huge blocky feet and at his face which was hardly like a human countenance. Frostbite had left a scab upon his hard dry skin.

"Nombre de Dios!" one of them cried. "Where have you come from?"

Guillaumet stared at the man blankly. His mind didn't want to work. Then he remembered and he turned slowly and looked up at the mountains. The crags of the Andes loomed above.

"Up there," Guillaumet muttered. "Somewhere away up there."

The news flashed across Argentina: Guillaumet had been found! Guillaumet is alive. Saint Exupéry was having lunch between flights in a restaurant in Mendoza when a man stuck his head in the door and shouted:

"They've found Guillaumet!"

Then Saint Exupéry flew to San Rafael. In forty minutes he spotted an open car heading for Mendoza and he dropped down to buzz it. Guillaumet was in the car. They were bringing him down from San Rafael. Saint Exupéry landed alongside the road and ran to the car to embrace the friend he had thought was dead.

Guillaumet sat in the car in a fuzzy daze, his body shriveled and his hands and feet numb, his face burnt. He stared bleakly at Saint Exupéry.

"Guillaumet," Exupéry cried, "how did you do it?"

Guillaumet opened his mouth to try to describe the Herculean battle he had fought against the snows and crags. But it was too much to explain. So he said:

"What saves a man is to take a step. Then another step. It is always the same step, but you have to take it."

Then he closed his eyes and slept.

www.ingramcontent.com/pod-product-compliance
Lightning Source LLC
Chambersburg PA
CBHW050755250626
47155CB00005B/2065